UNFORESEEN SASKATCHEWAN

KEITH LANDRY

Copyright © 2023 by Keith Landry

All rights reserved.

No part of this book may be reproduced in any form or by any electronic or mechanical means, including information storage and retrieval systems, without written permission from the author, except for the use of brief quotations in a book review.

SASKATCHEWAN
Regina
Canada
MONTANA
NORTH DAKOTA
Miles City
MINNESOTA
SOUTH DAKOTA
United States
IDAHO
WYOMING
IOWA
NEBRASKA
NEVADA
UTAH
COLORADO
KANSAS
MISSOURI
OKLAHOMA
ARKANSAS
ARIZONA
NEW MEXICO
Las Cruces
TEXAS
LOUISIANA

CONTENTS

Introduction   vii

PART I

1. Allan Walker   3
2. Jose Kirk   15
3. Dr. Peter Wong   33
4. Big Muddy Murders   41
5. Corporal Lyle Jennings   49
6. Peter Hamilton   59
7. Rebecca Mahon   65
8. Walker Interviews Wong   77
9. Bill Larsen   91
10. President Harrison Petry   97
11. Mark Jackson   103
12. Ongoing Murder Investigation   119
13. Sammy Nelson   127
14. Temporary Stay   135
15. Podcasting   147

PART II

16. Hail Storm   155
17. Trappings   169
18. Wong's Decision   175
19. Goodbye to Miles City   183
20. Mr. Big   195
21. Tornado   209
22. Political Candour   215

PART III

23. Wong Walks Among the Spirits   231
24. Fall Encounters   239

25. Fake Science	249
26. Canada's Thanksgiving	255
PART IV	
27. Alberta Clipper	265
28. Freda's Interview	273
29. Present Threats	285
Epilogue	289
Acknowledgments	295
About the Author	297
Also by Keith Landry	301

INTRODUCTION

In Washington, DC:

"Damn," he said, "damn nuisance."

In the dark room, the other man was forced to listen to the rant of a man who was asserting power over him.

Trapped, he thought, *as a result of his own character flaw.*

"You only have to find out where he is. We'll look after the rest. Do you understand?" Menacingly, the man moved closer, within an inch of the distressed man's face.

Shouting now, he asked, "Do you understand?"

Ashen faced, near vomiting, the man bobbed his head up and down. Was it fear? It was; what else could it be?

Dreading what he was being asked to do. He had never done what the other man was demanding.

"We will pay off your gambling debts. But should you not succeed, I will harm you in ways you cannot imagine. Understand?"

The man's head bobbed up and down again. He understood only too well.

"Our information shows he's operating from an unknown location in Regina, Saskatchewan. You know the city well. You're from there.

"The man's using an alias. He goes by the name of Allan Walker. He has a very popular podcast. Do you know of him?"

The other man shook his head, "No."

"He's anti-everything. Spiels off about the antidemocratic movement in the United States, the oil and gas industry, the rights of Americans, and the threat of climate change. Fucking leftist! Wants us to share our power and wealth with those that haven't earned it."

The other man asked, "Why doesn't he still live in the States?"

"I thought you were so smart. Idiot! He knows I'm after him. Knows I want him dead."

"Why me?" The other man's voice quavered only slightly.

"Come on," the man said, "I have you by the balls. Your debtors are wanting their money. They'll treat you poorly if you don't pay. Remember how nice they were when you asked them for money. They have dual personalities—nice now, not so nice later. The only thing keeping them off your back is my cheque book.

"You're a renowned environmentalist. When Walker learns you're in Regina, he'll want you on his podcast. You will get close and confirm that he's my man.

"I want you to keep me informed. You can Zoom me from Regina. There is a two-hour time difference between Washington and Regina, so Zoom me around ten Regina time."

"Sure," replied the man. Not knowing what he meant with his sure—sure, he'd keep in touch, sure he'd meet Walker, but he wasn't sure he could be party to a murder conspiracy.

Meanwhile in Ottawa, Ontario

The Canadian Prime Minister greeted the Indian Prime Minister and welcomed him to her parliamentary office. It was a meeting between two Commonwealth countries that were part of the five leading economies of the world. India's economy was now, in the year 2032, just behind the United States, which had the largest economy in the world.

China had fallen to third place because of its aging population and its failure to harness cleaner sources of energy. Air pollution due to gas-powered vehicles and coal-generating electricity had resulted in China having lower birth rates and higher mortality rates from respiratory diseases. The cost of air pollution on the Chinese economy since 2022 had risen fivefold to an estimated 6 trillion dollars. Lower worker productivity, lower crop yields, and higher health costs were the main contributors of the sagging economy.

The effects of China's warming climate had resulted in droughts and extraordinary storms that caused flooding, ruined rice and grain crops, and killed people. If the storms didn't kill them, starvation did. China's workforce had shrunk, and many older people retired or died, which had cut into China's ability to staff important growth industries. China's successful invasion and occupation of Taiwan had proved to be very expensive, which also contributed to China's fall.

On the other hand, India's workforce was young, well-educated, and skilled. Its democratic government modernized how business operated in the country by scrapping fossil fuel subsidization and shifting the subsidies to renewable energy sources. Small business provided the opportunities for creative entrepreneurship and employed most of its young workforce.

In 2015, India was listed as the fourth highest contributor to climate change. But the Indian leaders embraced challenging carbon dioxide emission targets and took the action necessary to achieve those targets.

Some world economists believe that India will overtake the United States as the largest economy by 2050. These economists base their projection on the right-wing agenda of the Patriots of America Party (PAP), which deny the existence of global warming and is tearing away at the fabric of the American democracy in such a way.

"Mr. Prime Minister, I understand that, before we sign our trade agreement, you wish to discuss visa applications for Indian students to attend Canadian universities," stated the female Prime Minister of Canada.

"That's right. Currently there are 200,000 of our young people attending your post-secondary schools. Many are having trouble renewing their annual visa permits because of your immigration backlogs. Are there ways we can assist in speeding up the process at our end? These students are from our more affluent families. Their parents are clamouring at my doorstep to fix things. Of course, I tell them it's a Canadian problem." But the Canadian Prime Minister knew he was really telling her to speed up the process or there would be repercussions. That's how diplomacy was, tit for tat.

The Canadian Prime Minister responded, "Let's have my immigration minister meet with your officials and see how we can improve the issue by working together."

"Thank you, Madame Prime Minister. There is one more matter on immigration that I wish to address."

"Yes, Mr. Prime Minister, and what is that?" she asked.

"Our young students here in your country often aspire to remain in Canada upon graduation. With over a billion people in my country, it's admirable that you offer these students permanent resident status upon graduation if they find work. However, your backlog is resulting in recent graduates having to return to India because they have not received the permanent resident documents. That's placing a financial burden on them, which is most often borne by their parents."

"Mr. Prime Minister, I'm well aware of the problem. Canadian employers who've offered these students work are clamouring at my doorstep as well."

She continued, "Our economic success, from the 10th largest economy only ten years ago to the 5th today, has dealt with many labour market problems. Workers are in high demand, particularly the demand for higher skilled workers. Our country issued 432,000 permanent resident permits in 2022. This year, we expected that number to be one million. We're hiring more immigration officers and implementing faster application and approval processes by using new technologies. But, like other Canadian businesses, we're having recruitment issues. I'm so grateful for your offer of help. Hopefully our folks can find solutions.

"Now for the agreement on India to purchase Canadian-made electric batteries for your cars and other manufacturing uses, I ask if the terms are agreeable to India?"

Ten years earlier, Canada had built the world's largest homegrown lithium electric battery supply chain. Canada was the only democratic nation having the essential raw minerals. China was Canada's biggest competitor. However, after their invasion and occupation of Taiwan, other democratic nations preferred dealing with Canada.

This new Canadian industry, which required billions in government and private investment, had created thousands of jobs in every province. The main manufacturing infrastructure was located in southern Ontario. This region already had an established automotive parts and assembly manufacturing capacity, which was re-purposed for the new product line.

The new industry added 90 billion dollars to the Canadian economy in 2031. Batteries are the centre of the green economy. They power our transportation, provide lights for our homes, and warm up our offices.

The Indian Prime Minister smiled and said, "Yes, we are satisfied with the proposed terms."

PART I

SPRING 2032

1

ALLAN WALKER
REGINA, SASKATCHEWAN

The studio was located in one of Regina's oldest neighbourhoods named the Al Ritchie. Located just east of the downtown core, the homes in this area were built in the early to mid -20th century.

The studio was where Allan Walker created his controversial podcasts for his North American following, which now exceeded 1 million listeners a week. From 100 to 1 million in five years. What a ride on a monster wave!

It was years earlier that Walker had left the United States to live in Canada, ultimately settling in the prairie city of Regina, Saskatchewan.

He used false documents to enter as a visitor and then disappeared off the radar of the Canadian immigration authorities. Prior to coming to Canada, Walker had stopped drinking.

He had been a top Washington reporter on CNN until they reluctantly fired him. His employer could not tolerate his frequent bouts of on-air impairment with slurred words and disjointed interviews.

He now used his journalism skills to earn a living in Regina. His success had risen following his virulent attacks on the President of the United States and his mob-like party, the Patriots of America Party (PAP). Exposing them was his *raisin d'être*.

Mainstream broadcasting from a network like CNN or Fox News still dominated the way most people received their information. Fox, as a purveyor of misinformation, played a significant role in PAP's ability to gain and maintain power in much of the United States. CNN, once the respected leader providing most Americans their news, lost viewers as older, white people turned to watch Fox News. There they heard what they wanted to hear. CNN reported more of the facts; but with a significant decline in viewers, it had become far less effective combatting the false narratives spewed by Fox and the increasing presence of right-wing digital podcasts.

Walker saw a righteous cause that provided an enormous business opportunity. He'd fight the bastards ruining his beloved country. Focusing on the younger, more progressive, he found a audience more in tune with and accepting of an ever-changing world.

In the day when he was one of CNN's top White House correspondents, he chased down the truth about politics and politicians like a lion hunting its prey. Walker also ran with the wrong crowd. Drinking in bars each evening became like a mouse bait station for him. It had one opening, a one-way entry point that blocked any exit. There was poison inside that the mouse ate and died from. For Walker, alcohol was his poison and unless he found an escape, he was going to die from it.

He chased a story about an anonymous rich man's corruption in Washington. He revealed it all to the public. The story set off an investigation by the Federal Bureau of Investigation (FBI) that resulted in the man's incarceration.

That terrific piece of journalism forced Walker to flee Washington. The man he exposed was vengeful. It also forced Walker to face his drinking problem.

A sober man, a man to serve a cause, a resolute man, an enemy of the powerful and corrupt, Walker was at peace with himself.

He eyed the headline of the New York Times. It read:

Effects of the Rise of Far-Right Politics

Throughout the world, political re-emergence of the far-right movements in democracies is continuing. Some of these movements have even gained power in some countries. In our own country, Harrison Petry, a wealthy white man, has taken the party of Lincoln, our once-dominant Republican Party and made it redundant. Supported by like-minded individuals, he formed the Patriots of America Party (PAP). These Americans wish to have the Office of the President of the United States wield authoritarian power, suppress opposition, and implement ultranationalist political ideology and policies. They assault individual freedoms and rights to sow more power for the rich and prominent.

Eight years ago, Petry won the 2024 presidential election. The same 2024 election saw PAP win both the House of Representatives and the Senate.

Since then, PAP has moved to implement policies and legislation to reduce or eliminate social security benefits, in place to assist poorer Americans. PAP, pointing to the crime surge resulting from increases in poverty, increased police funding and supported tough police responses. People of colour were being stopped without cause and if they resisted, they were arrested. Weekly, news outlets reported police beatings or shootings of people of color on the streets of cities across America for resisting arrest.

The cruelest action taken by this cruel governing White House and Congress was the total repeal of the Obama Health Care Act, causing 75 million Americans to lose health insurance.

His appointments early in his tenure of two ultra-conservative judges to the Supreme Court has boosted the President's anti-democratic agenda. The two joined four conservatives appointed by republican presidents, giving a six to three majority for conservatives. Petry uses the Supreme Court to lend legitimacy to his activities.

Throughout the south and central part of the country, legislatures with tenable relationships with Petry have rolled back 70 years of progressive laws that were intended to promote an egalitarian society.

Petry and PAP have used rhetoric and aggression against legal and illegal immigrants from Central American and Mexico, wanting to escape violence and poverty in their own countries, as a rallying point for their partisan followers. 'Lock em up, separate the children, and go back where you came from' have been Petry's shout-outs at rallies, sending crowds into a frenzy. He has blamed high crime rates on the illegal residents.

Petry and his followers have lulled Americans into complacency. PAP told them that liberal ideas were the source of their grievances, that liberals helped minorities at the expense of conservatism. People bought the lies and then lost their right to vote. It was the disenfranchised election law that the federal government passed that awoke the average American to what was happening. Some of these losers were poor white voters who had once supported Petry's agenda.

The new federal election law states that only a Christian person who owns property worth $100,000 or has assets worth that can vote in federal elections. The Supreme Court upheld the law. Their reasoning was that the country's founders meant for only privi-

leged people to vote. The president cruised to a second term in office.

American politics has always been about big money and to whom it goes. It divides donations from the wealthy between PAP and the Democrats. But Petry receives enormous contributions from his individual followers besides the big money that funds conservatism.

With the legislative power behind him and backed by large amounts of money and an ultra-conservative Supreme Court, Petry has little resistance to push back against any policies he sought to advance. Made from the same self-centred and selfish cloth and as loud as Trump was, he was even more dangerous—he was smart.

For example, President Petry defunded the Internal Revenue Service (IRS). The IRS fell behind on revenue collection and its investigation of individuals and businesses that were failing to pay what they owed. This has been very popular with Petry's followers and reduced the government's ability to pay down the national debt, fund the social security net, or fund important climate change initiatives. The president uses the thinner purse as a reason to legislate reduced government expenditures on social programming and to shrink the size of government.

President Petry openly derides calls for action to fight climate change. Instead, his government, along with state governments following conservative agendas, support the fossil extraction industries like coal mining and oil and gas production. His govern-

ment also deregulates industries' carbon emission reduction obligations. These government actions received support from the Supreme Court. And, national budgets stopped including financial rewards to businesses, home owners, and the fossil industry, who attempted to reduce energy use or seek additional energy sources to combat global warning. Public research into alternative energy sources dwindled, leaving under-funded nongovernmental organizations to seek ways and means to stop the country from reaching the point of no return.

The impact of these ultra-conservative policies has been dreadful. Shrinking was not something most Americans considered when they thought of their beloved country. But by 2032, things in the United States have been shrinking. The American coastlines are retreating as the warming oceans claim land. Good farm land is shrinking as heatwave after heatwave dry up the soil. Fresh water for human consumption and for agriculture is becoming scarcer in the southwest. Deforestation, once caused by human harvesting timber, is now caused by wild forest fires that threaten towns and cities. Reduced precipitation contributes to water shortages. Wildlife is moving from land they lived on for centuries to alternative places where they can survive. Some wildlife that cannot move perish from the fires or from hunger and thirst.

Food is becoming scarcer because of the mega drought. Corn, grains, potatoes, vegetables, and fruit are scarcer and prices for them are higher. Many of the so-called working class and the poor cannot afford three square meals a day. They lose jobs to drought. But jobs are also lost in the fossil fuel industries not because of *actions to close them but because coal, gas, and oil supplies are running out in parts of the country. Fossil fuel is a non-renewable resource.*

Gross national production is down in the United States because of the impact of climate change, persistent inflation, and a population that is on the move from the southwest to cooler areas in the northeast, north central, and the northwest. Relocated companies cannot quickly replace huge production losses in the southwest. The biggest loss to Americans is the loss of abundant food crops, once so prevalent in places like California.

The wealthy and upper middle class buy properties in the northern parts of the United States. Manufacturers move plants north. It is the poorer in the southwest areas who cannot afford to move north in their own country. North to Canada is their only option. And Canada needs both skilled and unskilled workers.

Please recall the tumultuous United States-Mexican border crossing problems during the Trump years. These problems have moved north to cluster at the United States-Canadian border. Americans gather at the border awaiting legal entry into Canada. Temporary communities spring up. Some migrants cross the border illegally.

Many of these working-class folks migrate north to western Canada. Some of these unfortunate people were the same ones who had thrown their lot in with the PAP.

Walker understood his mission. It was monumental.

Walker produced podcasts informing Americans about what was happening and encouraging peaceful civil disobedience to protest the loss of a democracy's most fundamental right and responsibility, the citizen's right to vote. Regrettably, if people would've exercised that right in the 2024 election in greater numbers, Petry might have lost. But poor turnouts weighed heavily in his favour. Now, in 2032, Petry was running for a third term because of PAP's success in challenging the two-term limit as unconstitutional. The Supreme Court ruled term limits were in fact unconstitutional. Those privileged enough to vote supported Petry.

Walker organized his notes for his April 1st podcast to be released on the internet at 6 PM to his Canadian and American English-speaking audiences.

The time was 10 AM. It takes hours to complete a podcast for release. He'd start by doing an initial run. After his first review, he'd edit and edit until he was satisfied that the piece was ready for release.

As usual, Walker released his podcast at 6 PM Central Time. He started by welcoming his audience and providing them with a temperature analysis from different locations around the world.

"Good evening, folks, from Regina, Saskatchewan, Canada. Heat is the leading weather killer on earth. And our planet is heating up. It's only April, and the United Kingdom is experiencing midday temperatures in the twenties of Celsius.

That's 8 degrees higher than ten years ago. This is the fourth day in a row of these record temperatures.

"My fellow Americans, do you know that Hispanic refugees who entered the United States illegally are journeying north to Canada? They've journeyed beyond Texas, Oklahoma, Kansas, Colorado, and New Mexico because after their dangerous travel from Central America, they're finding ICE (Immigration and Custom Enforcement) relentlessly hunting them down. Many, to avoid capture and deportation, keep on the move north to Canada. Just this past year, ten thousand have made their way into Saskatchewan. They enter illegally from North Dakota and Montana.

"Now, my fellow countrymen, Canada had a Third Country Agreement with the United States. That agreement allowed Canada to return these refugees back to the United States because they could find safety there. So why has Saskatchewan ten thousand of these refugees finding safety here?

"Because … because … now, this is a fact … a Canadian judge ruled that the United States is no longer safe for these asylum seekers. The judge, a member of Canada's federal court, declared the agreement invalid.

"This is what your ultraconservative, right-wing government is doing to our beloved country. It is becoming a pariah among free democratic countries.

"These are people fleeing despots, violence, hunger, and global warming, and our own country hunts and deports them with malice.

"But that's not the only people seeking refuge in Saskatchewan. There are thousands of your fellow Americans waiting at the Saskatchewan border to immigrate to Canada.

"Canadian Immigration officials have opened an office in Miles City, Montana, five hours south of here. This is the newest one added to the scores of others in localities across the northern United States. These offices facilitate processing immigration applications to Canada because of the number of people at the United States-Canada border who wish to come to Canada.

"Just a few years ago, there were only a handful of Americans wanting to seek refuge in Canada. The number is now in the thousands. So large is the number that Canadian immigration authorities inform us application processing is taking almost a year. These new immigrants, fellow Americans, are from the once great states of Colorado, Texas, Oklahoma, and New Mexico.

"Imagine, Miles City, Montana, with a permanent population of 7,000 now has almost 3,000 American migrants living temporarily in and around the city. A farming and ranching hub on the I94 east-west highway and 5 hours south of Regina, Mile City's population is declining because farms and ranches are being deserted. Heat and dried up soil has taken its toll. City folks are also moving on.

"Our United States government has allowed climate change to destroy people and their communities. Now, it does nothing to help these people forced to migrate. If you haven't yet, please read John Steinbeck's wonderful novel "The Grapes of Wrath." In the novel, Americans migrate due to drought and economic hardship in the Great Depression from Oklahoma to California in search of jobs, land, dignity, and a future. Government authorities like the police ally with the wealthy growers to suppress hopeless migrants. It's history repeating itself. You must not allow this to happen. Join a non-violent resistance organization today."

At the end, Walker informed his listeners that a prominent climate change scientist would be joining him for several future podcasts.

2

JOSE KIRK
LA CRUCES, NEW MEXICO

A darkly tanned man dressed in clean, blue denim jeans, a sharp Cuban collar shirt, and a fedora straw hat stood in a voting line in the upper middle-class district of High Range, La Cruces, New Mexico. His dress was typical for Hispanic people living in southern New Mexico, near the Mexican border. His black hair and dress exposed his ancestry.

Jose Kirk mused that the four-hour wait in the long lineup to vote in the state election was something an American citizen should do to show the people whose intent was to suppress voting rights that it wouldn't work. It was only a few years ago that voters could vote at the many poll stations throughout the city, which were positioned to make it convenient for everyone. In those days, you could even mail your vote in. But the governing PAP removed poll stations in districts where poorer people lived, believing that most residents would not vote because of the new financial eligibility requirements and the need to have a photo ID.

Jose said to himself, "I've the financial means to register as a voter in the election. I've the right."

Jose's father was a white man who served in the marines. They had deployed him twice to active combat in Afghanistan in the early 21st century. His mother entered the United States some forty-plus years ago. She sought refuge in La Cruces. Congress's amnesty in 2000 provided her with the right to remain legally in the United States.

The sound of drums tore him from his thoughts. Under a haze of smoke from a nearby mountain fire, Jose could see the orange-red sun but, because of the murky air, he could not yet see where the drumming was coming from.

There was more noise, this time with people yelling obscenities and others pleading to leave them alone. The drumming and yelling came closer, moving up from along the rear of the line.

Jose scanned the horizon. From out of the haze appeared a soldier followed by about a dozen other soldiers, all marching on percussion to the menacing beat of their drums. They wore military attire from different eras of American history. Jose knew who they were. Members of PAP's militia, who called themselves *Pledging Allegiance*, were there to make trouble for the blacks and Hispanics intending to vote.

Jose tried to hide by turning away, to no avail. Someone from the group shouted, "Look over there. There's a wetback with the fedora on his greasy black hair."

Another shouted, "Get out of the line!"

Jose did not move. Two men pushed people out of way to grab and pull Jose out of the line. Jose, mindful that no one was coming to his rescue, did not fight back.

"What the fuck are you doing in the line?" hollered, a man wearing raggedy denims. Jose could smell cheap booze and stale cigarette on him. He was tall and thin with scruffy blond hair.

Jose pushed the man's hand away and replied defiantly, "I'm exercising my right to vote. Do you have that right?"

The man was taken aback, "Uh … fuck if I need to. Are you being uppity with me? Get out and go home or else."

"Or else what?" asked Jose, who was stiffening with resolve. This was an assault on his freedom.

Another man who had been standing behind Jose flicked the fedora off Jose's head. When Jose bent to retrieve it, the beating started. Jose regained consciousness in a local hospital.

He smelled Freda's sweetness first. Then he smelled antiseptic and piss and pus and dried blood. The smells jarred him awake.

"How long ... how long have I been out?" Jose asked in Spanish.

Freda smiled at him and answered in Spanish. She kept fussing over the dark hair that was falling over his eyes. "You've been unconscious since the attack."

A La Cruces detective came into his room, and Jose reported what happened. The detective advised that no one had come forward to make a statement, and no one appeared to have videoed the incident.

"We'll do what we can, but an arrest seem unlikely," said the detective.

～

FREDA ENTERED the living room of their five-bedroom, five-bath Tuscan-style home. It was 4,000 square feet of luxurious living. They had it built five years earlier. At the front entrance to the house, there was beautiful stonework with an exceptional archway and a hand-carved door. The beautiful craftsmanship continued throughout the interior. In the living room there was a stone wood-burning fireplace with an oak mantle. The dining room had a hand-crafted oak buffet. Each room throughout the sprawling bungalow has eye-popping features. Freda had demanded quality, and Jose had consented to the additional costs for it.

"Jose, can I get you anything?" she asked her husband who was convalescing on a chesterfield.

"No, thank you, my dear."

Freda looked at the man with whom she had fallen in love when he first came to pick up her father for work. Her father was a supervisor for the fledging landscaping business Jose ran.

Jose had been sullen since the attack. It hurt him more emotionally than physically. This sweet and gentle man had strived to better himself. He had believed that if he were successful, he would be comfortable in any social setting. Money was supposed to speak loudly, the great equalizer. But that was just bullshit! The louses who beat him and blocked him from voting had put him in his place. No one helped him, and no one had come forward. Justice was just a pipe dream for many people in America. Jose knew he would always be a wetback, even though he had been born here.

But even before the beating, his life had begun a downward spiral. The once flourishing landscaping business was threatened by water restrictions that caused many of his customers with irrigation maintenance contracts to turn to xeriscaping. Xeriscaping is a type of water-conserving landscaping that aimed to reduce or even eliminate the reliance on supplemental water from irrigation. The companies doing xeriscaping were larger businesses employing college graduates to design and install landscaping for their customers.

Jose had lost roughly 50 percent of his maintenance contracts and rarely received a call to install a new irrigation system.

Freda, who lived under the constant fear of being part of an Immigration and Custom Enforcement (ICE) roundup of illegals, was not a citizen. With PAP in power, roundups were more frequent. This weighed heavily on the minds of the couple.

Jose was a man whose focus was on family and work. Freda had the same goals, but she was more learned about what was happening elsewhere. Where Jose saw trees, Freda saw forests. Having foresight, she planned to share with Jose her thoughts on what they needed to do next.

"Freda, have you gone mad? They have polar bears on streets that have snow on the ground year around. Do they even have running water and electricity? Canada, Sas..kat..che..wan, where's that?" asked an incredulous Jose.

"Seriously, Jose, polar bears, running water, electricity? It's as advanced or more advanced than New Mexico."

She showed him her iPhone. On the screen was a job ad for a seasonal landscaper in Regina, Saskatchewan. It was for the University of Regina. For the other part of the year, the hired person could stay on doing maintenance for the student residences. Starting pay was $30.00 an hour with benefits like vacation leave, dental care, sick leave, etc.

"Now Jose, the pay rate is in Canadian dollars. That means it's about $22 an hour in US currency. But it's a start. We'd be bringing money with us. And I will have the same path to citizenship as you and the kids."

"Twenty-two dollars an hour! I've made three times that in good years. Why would I live with polar bears, knee deep in snow for that?" snorted Jose.

Freda showed Jose an article from USA Today that ranked the best countries in the world. Canada was number one. The article used factors like quality of life, good job market, political stability, affordability, well-developed health and education systems, and progressive action to combat climate change in determining rankings.

Freda said, "Do you see the United States in the top ten? No, you don't. The last time it was in the top ten was ten years ago. That was before the ultraconservatives started to run this country."

Jose reread the article. He hemmed and hawed before replying. Then he said, "Let me think about it."

"Jose, I hate what happened to you. But it happens to me all the time. You're lighter skinned than I am. I'm affected by subtle racism everywhere I go, except when I'm among the Mexican community. I also fell into the trap of thinking that owning this house, driving an expensive car, and wearing nice jewelry would make us more accepted by the city's elite. It doesn't.

"But Jose, my greatest fear is that it's only going to get worse because of the extreme heat and continuing drought. Sooner than later, people are going to fight each other for clean water and food. History has shown that minorities lose every time that happens."

The wind picked up around supper time. Freda looked out their front window. She saw dust and debris swirling about. From the west, a wall of dust a mile high and many miles wide was rolling toward the city. In minutes it swallowed the downtown. Freda could no longer see the city. A haboob, a dust storm, had almost reached their neighbourhood.

Pointing to the approaching dust storm, she called Jose to hurry and bring all the lawn furniture into the garage. She drove their vehicles inside. They closed all the windows and vents and turned off the air conditioning.

Their children, Manuel and Victoria, were directed to the protected centre of the house where Jose and Freda joined them.

From deep inside the house, they could hear the strong winds and sand and debris hitting the outside walls and roof.

Within 10 minutes, a thunderstorm replaced the mile high wall of dust.

This was the third haboob in a month. The soil of the land surrounding the city was so dry from the years of drought. High winds lifted up the topsoil and spread it over areas miles away. This storm killed three people in a 19-car pileup on I25.

∼

SITTING among his family and friends, 40-year-old Jose Kirk's mind wandered from the conversation and festivities at their going-away fiesta.

Things were so different a few years back, he thought to himself. He had been a successful businessman. At its peak, his landscaping business had hundreds of residential contracts and many employees.

Most of his workers did not have a green card, which was required to work legally in the United States. He could've underpaid them and been unconcerned about their plight. But no, Jose was principled. He paid fair wages and looked after them, ensuring they received any needed medical help. Often, he shared their medical costs from out of pocket. His parents had taught him responsibility toward the less fortunate. His mother impressed on him that people should not go hungry because of where they were born or the colour of their skin.

This going-away fiesta was for Jose and his family. After weeks of deliberating Freda's relocation proposal, he agreed with her that it would be best to go. He had applied for the university's landscaping position and got it. The university put in motion the process to sponsor his immigration to Canada.

Jose smelled the smoke in the air. Smoke was moving in from massive forest fires in Lincoln National Park. Today, the Lincoln National Park was the source; other days it was from the Gila National Forest. The smoke might also originate from the abundant grass fires that were threatening homes on the outskirts of La Cruces. It was hot and the fires were always stoked by the strong winds. Fortunately, there were no blackouts from the fires today.

"Keep your fingers crossed," he sighed.

La Cruces is 41 miles from the Mexican border on I25, a north-south freeway and 225 miles south of Albuquerque. La Cruces is within the eco-regions of the Chihuahuas desert. The city's water source depends on the Rio Grande river. With a ten-year drought and extreme heat, water flow and supply from the Rio Grande has been dropping year after year. Area ranching and farming competed for water with the 200,000 plus people living in La Cruces and surrounding communities.

God damn climate change, thought Jose. It took few brains to know something bad was happening on this planet. Yet Freda tells him that the PAP candidates are convincing people it's a far-left conspiracy. Lame-brained people are buying the notion that it's a natural phenomenon and nothing can be done about it. This is being told despite New

Mexico being the 6th fastest place in the United States heating up. It's Freda who keeps him on what's going on. She follows those things. Jose just wants to work and provide for his family.

He had confronted local politicians when they rang his doorbell during election campaigns that they were short-sighted in restricting homeowners' water use for trees and plants. He believed they were allowing the soil to erode from a lack of moisture. He had learned in high school science that plants and trees draw in carbon dioxide, break down and store the carbon, and breathe oxygen back into the atmosphere. If they had just allowed homeowners to maintain green surroundings, the homeowners would be able to spend time outside in shaded country-like spaces instead of inside running the A/C at full throttle and wasting energy that uses water to generate it. Apartment dwellers needed green spaces to get out of their hot apartments instead of running those little A/C units that use so much energy. Most of the city's source of energy was from crude oil and natural gas, resulting in greenhouse gas emissions. They need enormous amounts of water for converting oil and gas to energy. Restrict old A/C usage, and it'll get people outdoors. That's what Jose believed.

"Wouldn't it make sense," he asked a PAP candidate running for the State Senate, "for the government to provide incentive to farmers, ranchers, businesses, developers, and homeowners to reduce their carbon footprint?"

Freda had told him all about carbon footprints. A carbon footprint is the total amount of greenhouse gas (including carbon dioxide and methane) that is generated by an individual's actions.

The PAP candidate told him he was being hoodwinked. "People need a growing economy for better-paying jobs. That growth depends on crude oil, natural gas, and coal. That's our state's strength; we have lots of it."

"You piece of shit, my business is closed because of water shortages. For God's sake, there's smoke in the air all the time and people from here are going north because of these things, and you stand before me telling me I'm being hoodwinked. Get the fuck off my porch," growled Jose.

"Why," he asked himself, "do I have to be the one who pays a higher price from this so-called global warming?"

"Hey Jose, here's a beer," said his best friend, Oscar Munoz. Oscar sat down on the empty lawn chair beside Jose.

Jose snapped out of his woolgathering, took the beer in hand, and said, "Thank you, my friend."

Oscar smiled at Jose and said, "Amigo, I'm sure gonna miss you. I'd join you if it weren't for my folks needing me and Maria to care of them. A trip that far with so much uncertainty would near kill them. Ah ... that's not the only reason. You know me, prefer to stick with what I know rather than head out to a place I know little about. God, I've rarely ever left the county except to go south across the border to see what family I have left there."

"Oscar, I hope I'm doing right by my family. When my folks moved to Wisconsin five years ago, they could afford to buy property there. In fact, I gave them money to help them. Five years ago, I could afford to. Business was steady, money was coming in. Today my business is worthless; my trucks and equipment sold for 50 cents on the dollar and my five-year-old home sold for less than it cost me to build.

"My parents asked us to move in with them until I found employment. But what's a guy like me gonna do in an area where you need a college degree in a profession or a trade in demand? And I'm a man, after all, 40 years old. I'm not moving back in with my retired parents.

"No, this place with the long name, Saskatchewan, seems a better option than someplace in the northern United States where only people with educations or a trade can have a future.

"Freda told me Saskatchewan has many of the natural resources the rest of the fucked-up world needs. The province has closed most oil, gas, and coal production. Lithium deposits in the province have resulted in the province having one of the largest capacities for car battery production in the world. And, it's not very populated and has a significant shortage of workers. And they grow lots of grain. Bread has gotta be good there."

Oscar looked confused. "Okay, what's a province?"

Jose laughed, "You think I really know? A province is like a state, I guess. Don't matter cause I heard Canadians are polite. At least, that's what Freda tells me. And they don't have people rioting and burning down inner cities over cops shooting coloured folks 35 times in the back and then saying they were defending themselves. That means more to me than understanding how their government works."

A large dog with a lot of shepherd in it came panting toward Jose with a 12-year-old girl and a 9-year-old boy following close on its heels. The dog sat beside Jose, who fondly petted the old grey head.

"Oh, Charlie, are these two young ones chasing you in this heat? Near 80 degrees. Kids, don't pick on this old dog. He'll have a heart attack," quipped Jose.

~

THREE DAYS LATER, Jose worked outside with his daughter Victoria packing a U-Haul trailer. He had bought it second hand from a junk dealer. It required new tires and some new utility taillights. Jose did the maintenance himself. Then he hooked it behind his 12-year-old gas-guzzling Dodge Durango. He had sold his fancy cars and kept this vehicle. It was roomy, and it could pull the U-Haul.

They were taking what they could fit in the trailer and the Durango. He used 40-ounce stainless steel jerry cans for drinking water. Because of the drought, he wasn't sure how easily accessible drinking water would be on the trip. Plastic bags and bottles had been banned several years earlier by the Environmental Protection Agency, which is why he was using the jerry cans.

"Hey, Freda, can you bring out the frozen food in the cooler so I can put it in the mid-section of the trailer?" They had packed a pre-chilled cooler tightly with dry ice bags in order to bring some food essentials. They should be in Miles City, Montana, in two days. He had rented a house there for a short-term stay. The frozen food should be okay until they reached the rental house and could put the contents in the home freezer.

Charlie wagged his tail, anticipating his ride in the Durango. He couldn't know that he'd never return here. The children knew and understood. Leaving friends and childhood memories is never easy. But after weeks of knowing their departure was inevitable, they bravely gave into the notion of relocating.

It was different for their mother. Freda had wept all night in her beloved home. She cried over leaving her mother and father and her siblings and their families. Freda was sad. But it had been her idea, her plan, and her intuition that life would be better for them in Saskatchewan. A quest for a better life for them pushed her to give up what they had in

La Cruces. And, in Canada, she could someday be a Canadian citizen. She would no longer fear the sound of ICE agents knocking at their door.

Oh, she had tried. Tried so hard to convince her family to join them on their journey. But her family could not envision being so far from Mexico. There were after all family members still there. Freda tried to tell them they couldn't ever chance a visit there. They were illegals in the U.S., and if they left, they'd have to sneak back in to return. Her family could not be convinced. They'd take their chances that ICE agents would not find them in La Cruces.

Freda brought out the cooler.

"Jose, go in and turn off the power and water. Victoria and I will finish packing. Call Manuel to get out here and get into the vehicle. Do a final check while you're inside to make sure we forgot nothing."

Jose did as he was told. Inside, he found Manuel and sent him out to the car. Emotions gripped Jose as he shut off the power and water and made his final check of their home. Five years earlier, they had moved into their dream home in this middle-class neighbourhood. The new home had been a symbol of how their hard work achieved the American dream. Now, the dream was lost and memories were bitter.

He locked the front door as he left the cool interior, then placed the key in the realtor's lock box. Freda was bent over displaying her shapely keister. *Wow,* he thought, *I'm such a lucky guy; my wife is such a smart and beautiful woman.*

Everyone, including Charlie, got into the car. The big dog poked his head out the back passenger window. The two children sat in the back with him.

Jose drove from his neighbourhood to the I25 and turned onto the north ramp bearing the large sign, "Albuquerque 225 miles."

The children were on their tablets. Freda listened to Spanish music on her smart sunglasses. Jose drove and wondered what lied ahead for them.

Jose and Freda had received a decent offer for their home despite it being a buyers' market. They were headed to Miles City, Montana, where he could rent a home on a monthly basis, no lease involved. They did not know what condition it would be in but hoped it would be decent.

There was a Canadian Immigration office in Miles City, so Jose could check regularly on updates on the status of his permanent residency documents.

The plan for the first day on the road was to drive to Albuquerque and stay overnight with his brother Raoul and family.

3

DR. PETER WONG
REGINA, SASKATCHEWAN

Doctor Peter Wong, a man in his early 70s, stepped outside of the terminal of the small Regina Airport. The terminal faced north. The sun shone from the east, peaking above a pretty city skyline of high-rise office and apartment buildings. It was 9 AM on a crisp April morning.

He hailed a taxi. An electrically powered car pulled up to the curb. The driver jumped out, took Wong's luggage, and placed it in the trunk.

"The university, please," said Wong.

"What building?"

"Front door to the main campus will be fine, thank you," Wong replied.

The drive took Wong south down Lewvan Drive to the Ring Road and entered the Ring Road where a sign read, "East to Winnipeg." When another sign read "Wascana Parkway," the cab turned north and drove a short distance to where a large stone sign read, "The University of Regina." The cab turned right into the university entrance. The drive took only 10 minutes. Regina was not a big city like London, England.

London had been hot, 30C when he left. Unbelievable for an April day. But it had also struck him how warm it was when he stepped out of the air terminal. It sure wasn't like the Regina he grew up in. Most Aprils were still cold, some with six-foot snow banks. There was no sign of snow now.

After he paid the cabbie, he stood outside the entrance and qualms overcame him. He was returning to a place that years ago provided him the pathway to leave Regina behind. There had been no nostalgia for him then. It had been nothing but a means to an end. The journey was not as important as the destination. He had worked hard to excel. And he did, earning a Rhodes Scholarship to Oxford, one of only eleven granted in Canada that year. Now he was returning, a somewhat less distinguished person than he ought to be.

Students walked alone or in small groups outside the building entrance. There was excitement in the air. The school year end was nearing. The warmer weather allowed an escape to the outdoors. The students paid no attention to the older man.

Wong laid his luggage down on the promenade outside the entrance. He stood looking at the university buildings spread out over many acres. Fifty years, that's how long it was since he received his undergraduate degree. Then he received the Rhode's Scholarship at Oxford that drew him away to England, where he earned his masters and doctorate degrees in science. Much had changed. The university was much larger, and there were far more buildings than before.

Old emotions repressed from being out of touch with Regina swirled within and numbed his soul. Stilling himself, he released the hidden memories. He grew up in Regina, son of Chinese parents. Canada's head tax had prevented Peter and his mother from coming to Canada. The head tax was an entry fee for Chinese people to come and work here. Chinese immigrants were the only racial group subjected to this tax. His father could not afford the tax for both him and his family. Peter joined his father only after his mother died in China.

Peter's father operated a Chinese restaurant on old South Railway Road. It was once located at the very north end of downtown Regina. There was the railroad station and tracks on the north side. On the south side, there were old hotels where guests shared toilets and slept in small box rooms. The hotels had taverns and restaurants. There was a long two-story building that housed a second-hand store, a shoe store, a furniture store, confectionery, and a Chinese restaurant. That was his dad's. They lived in humble quarters upstairs.

During the day, people shopped along South Railway. During the evening and late hours, it was where men found women and booze.

Today, it is called Saskatchewan Drive. A large downtown mall replaced that long two-storey building.

In the old days, racism against the Chinese was blatant everywhere. Peter tried to overcome his visible ethnicity with exemplary school grades and athleticism. It never worked. He had to leave Regina and his father behind.

Wong had always been more alone than not throughout his life. He had tried marriage several times but found intellectual flaws in his wives. He'd had affairs with female colleagues, but those ended often when intellectual debates broke out into screaming matches.

Wong drank in moderation. But he gambled extensively and compulsively. So much so that he was usually living from one weekly cheque to the next. Royalties from his books on the environment went to gambling as fast as his weekly paycheques.

Was that why he was returning home? That was a big part of it. With tenure at Oxford university and world prominence in his field, he could have stayed there until he died, even when others learned of his gambling addiction. But his spiral into darkness continued unabated. Change offered hope. Returning to his roots was an option. What did he have to lose anyway? He was at an age when most of his colleagues had retired.

His stopover in Washington, DC, on his trip from London to Regina, saw him visit the MGM National Harbour Casino. He was by himself. No one was looking over his shoulder while his losses mounted. He experienced swift exhilaration on the few occasions luck was with him but then a heavy swing to anxiety and depression when his luck vanished. Quickly, he was unsure of exactly how long it took, he lost $10,000.

The Casino's management escorted him to the office where they demanded he prove he could cover more losses. He could not. Peter was tapped out. Funds that he had planned would make life easier in Regina were gone. The management asked him to leave after he settled his losses.

There is a casino in Regina. It's on Saskatchewan Avenue across from the downtown mall that had replaced the old building housing his father's restaurant and their small apartment.

The government runs the Regina Casino. Funny how people refer to gambling as an illness. Gamblers need treatment. Yet, government is addicted to the revenue it generates. No one says aloud that the government is addicted and needs treatment?

Fortunately for the impoverished professor, the university was providing him with living quarters. The university president had been generous in her offer of compensation, which included housing. The university was making a lot of noise about him teaching there. He need not even do research, which he had tired of during his years at Oxford.

Time to meet the university president in person. He gathered his things and entered the main door. Later this afternoon he would be interviewed by a fella named Allan Walker. He'd nap for a while after his meeting with the president and then freshen up for the interview.

∽

WONG TOOK a cab to the Riverside Memorial Park Cemetery. He had some time before he needed to meet up with Walker. It had been a while since he paid his respects to his deceased father. They buried his father in the section of the cemetery where people of Chinese ancestry were laid to rest. Peter has never visited his mother's resting place. It is in China. He has never gone back to China.

When his father died in the 1980s, Peter had returned to Regina from England to bury him. His career was going very well, so he bought an expensive headstone that read that Wong Tai Man had sacrificed a lot so his son could be an honourable person.

Peter thought of those years when the two of them were living in the quarters above the restaurant. His father worked and smoked packs of non-filtered cigarettes while cooking. When the restaurant closed, he drank Five Star whiskey and smoked while playing poker with men from the Chinese community.

Peter always had food and shelter. His first language was Mandarin. That's what he and his father spoke to each other. As a boy, he worked at the restaurant. Whenever he and his father spoke about school, his father spoke to him in broken English. It was a deliberate message from father to son. To get ahead in Canada, speak English and go to school.

"Homework, do it. After, go to bed. On time at school. Walking to Central High is not so bad. Oh, the little cold won't kill you," and so on. His dad did not know how he did in school. For all he knew, Peter might be failing his grades. His dad could not read or write English.

Peter worked hard at the restaurant, almost from the start when his dad opened it in the late 1950s. He acted as a translator when white clientele were there. It wasn't a fancy place in a good part of town, so most of the customers were down and outers, but most paid their bills.

When Peter graduated primary school, his dad stood in the darkest place in the school auditorium to watch his son receive his diploma. His father did not want others to see him. It was the same when Peter graduated from Central

High and the University of Regina. His father refused to fly to Oxford when he earned his doctorate, even knowing Peter would pay his fare. He feared flying.

Even with the Rhode's Scholarship, Peter needed additional funds. Mr. Wong paid Peter an hourly wage from Grade 9 on. And when Peter first arrived at Oxford, he opened his luggage to find $10,000 in an envelope from his father. It was his dad's life savings.

Tears came to Peter's eyes when he remembered he had never told his dad he loved him. Yes, he wrote to his dad from England thanking him profusely. Someone in Regina must have read it for his father because it had been written in English. Peter could speak Mandarin but, he could not write it.

Love and gratitude did not mean as much to his father as knowing that his son had become respected and admired; Peter had become an honourable man.

Peter had come back occasionally to visit his dad and sleep overtop the restaurant. And when he did, Dr. Wong was required to help. His father still worked hard and smoked and drank whiskey while playing cards with his Chinese acquaintances as if nothing had changed. When Peter thought about that, he smiled.

The cab had waited for him. He returned to it and got in, and it drove away to Walker's studio.

4

BIG MUDDY MURDERS
SOUTHEAST SASKATCHEWAN

They moved cautiously in the night. There was no moon; it was pitch dark.

It was difficult to walk on the ground. The land they were crossing had steep slopes, ravines, and gullies. The ground was dusty with a lot of deep cracks. No one wanted to fall down into a rocky gully or ravine.

It was cold out. Before coming over the Canadian border into Saskatchewan into an area called the Big Muddy Valley, they had been warned to dress warmly. They did.

This area was badlands, known in the late 19th century as a good place for outlaws to hide out.

The previous evening, the family had snuck into Canada just west of highway 36. The highway crossed the US-Canada border where Saskatchewan and Montana meet. Few people live in the area. There are more large ranches in the area than small grain farms. The land is not fertile enough to grow grain.

The Montana Christian organization who assisted their trip to the border provided ample water and some food. Still, they rationed it because they were uncertain how far they would have to walk to reach a town called Willow Bunch. That's where people from the Christian group on the Canadian side awaited them. From there, they would be assisted north to Saskatoon.

The parents travelled with a nineteen-year-old daughter, a sixteen- and thirteen-year-old son, and their youngest, an eleven-year-old girl. They were brown skinned and originated in Central America. Weeks earlier, they had joined a migrant caravan that journeyed to the US border. They crossed illegally into the US. To avoid ICE agents, they continued north. People they met along the way told them about Saskatchewan. "There's plenty of work there. Canada's immigration system for refugees was fairer. Canada is a welcoming country." That's what they were told. That's what they believed.

Sleeping in hiding places during the day and walking during the night kept them safer from the risk of detection.

They stopped to rest at the side of a butte.

"Where's Camila?" the mother frantically called out. "She's not with us."

The father counted heads to make sure no one else was missing. He told his family to stay put. He was going to retrace their steps.

He set out on his own. He could hear his wife calling out, "Camila, Camila." The father wished he had told her to stay quiet. It might draw attention to them. The man walked until dawn. He did not find his missing daughter. He reluctantly turned back to rejoin the others.

The three brothers set off from the cave in the side of butte on their four-wheeled all terrain vehicles (ATVs). They had secured their automatic rifles inside the cave by burying them in the ground of the cave. Afterwards, they drank a few beers and chewed on beef jerky. The lads were careless and lazy. They didn't clean up after themselves.

The youngest was high on something. He didn't appear to know where he was. The oldest, the one in charge, growled at him to get his shit together. They were leaving.

A woman's voice calling for Camilla could be heard east of their location. The eldest brother pointed in the direction of the voice and waved his two brothers to head that way.

The Hispanic man heard a voice from where his family had been resting. It was a cruel voice. "What are you wetbacks looking for in these hills? You fucking snuck into the country, didn't you?"

The father had learned some English on their journey, but not enough to understand what was being said. But the tone was not friendly.

He had no choice but to reveal himself to them. Raising his hands in the air, he approached. There were three young men with rifles. They had been travelling on ATVs.

"Sin problemas, señor," said the father. ("No problem, mister.")

"Stop right there," shouted the man, pointing his rifle in the father's direction. The Hispanic man didn't understand the young man and continued toward his family.

The man pointing the rifle fired a shot above the father's head. The father understood that. He stopped.

"Well, well, if it isn't the leader of this pack of illegals," said the same man.

The terrified Hispanic man replied, "Por favor, no nos hagas daño." ("Please, don't hurt us.")

"Fucking speak English, you grease ball Mexican," continued the man, who appeared to be the oldest and the one in charge.

"No Mexicano." ("Not Mexican.")

The youngest man, the one high on drugs, moved toward the nineteen-year-old daughter. He put his hand on her breast and squeezed cruelly. "I'd like a little piece of this one."

"Por favor, no lo hagas, déjala," cried the mother. ("Please don't do it, leave her.")

From behind, the sixteen-year-old boy grabbed the man molesting his sister. His sister ran off into the darkness. Spinning the bad hombre around, he got hold of the man's wrist and tore off some sort of wrist band. The man raised his rifle and fired a shot at the boy. With horror and disbelief on his face, the boy held his stomach. Blood gushed from a wound there.

The mother screamed and went to her son. The same man who had shot her son raised his gun and shot the mother in the head. The father lunged at the man holding a rifle on him and wrestled the gun away; he was turning to shoot his son's and wife's killer when the leader of the intruders shot the father. He then turned and shot the motionless thirteen-year-old boy.

Pointing to his youngest brother who had groped the girl, the leader said, "Go get her and bring her back. No reason we can't have a little fun."

The sun was coming up. He ran after her. When he returned, she was not with him.

Looking at the leader, he said, "She jumped or fell into a ravine. Cracked her skull. She's dead."

The leader ordered the two others, "Look around; make sure nothing is left that might lead to us."

They were lazy sorts; they spent most of their lives doing things half-assed. They didn't look very hard.

They got on their vehicles and rode off.

The youngest girl, lost, wandered through the wilderness. Her father had been clear not to make noise, so she didn't call out. She drifted over the rough terrain, not knowing where her family was. She had no water or food, but she hoped that she would find them when daylight returned.

∼

The following morning, a man from Coronach was out in the Big Muddy riding his horse and came across the four bodies. There was no telephone reception out in the area, so he had to ride back to Coronach where a three-man Royal Canadian Mounted Police (RCMP) detachment was. The corporal-in-charge was Lyle Jennings.

Jennings and one of his men, Constable Stu Barnes, drove back out with the man. The Corporal checked the four dead. He noticed two sets of footprints on the dusty ground. He followed the prints and found a fifth body down in the ravine.

Jennings returned and told the others about his discovery.

"Stu, I'm going to get a recovery team and forensic experts out. I'll phone into Regina from the police radio in the car. Be back shortly."

After Jennings phoned in, he looked southwest with the sun at his back. He thought he saw movement. He used his binoculars. There was a tiny figure moving about some half mile away. He couldn't discern what it was so he walked toward it.

As he got closer, he could see that it was a child. "It's a young girl," he said to himself.

She looked tired and dirty. Dust covered her face, and she seemed disoriented. At the sight of the tall uniformed police officer, she fell to her knees and cried out in Spanish, "Mamá y papá."

Jennings approached her cautiously and said gently, "Little girl, you're safe now." He handed her his water container. She put it to her lips and drank thirstily.

He gestured that he wanted to lift her up in his arms. She nodded it was okay. Corporal Jennings picked her up, and she clasped her thin arms around his neck. He carried her away from where her family lay towards his police vehicle. Opening the passenger door, he tucked her inside and found a blanket to wrap around her slight frame. She said again, "Mamá y papá." Jennings had no reply for her. He sat in the driver's seat and used the radio phone again. "Please send an ambulance with a child protection worker."

He shouted out to his partner, "Stu, I'm staying in the car until the others come. Look around for clues but try not to disturb anything."

Constable Barnes leaned over and picked up a strange-looking wristband lying on the ground.

The man who'd found the bodies showed Barnes some ATV tracks.

5

CORPORAL LYLE JENNINGS
CORONACH, SASKATCHEWAN

Their bungalow has white painted siding. It is small, built in the 1970s. There are three small bedrooms, a large kitchen, a living room, and one full bathroom.

They use the back door as their usual entry point. It leads into the kitchen. Outside, there is a cement pad for two cars to park on. Lyle is paid quite well. They can afford more. But RCMP members know better than to buy a nice home in rural detachments in such a small community. Rural real estate is difficult to resell. The young couple rent this home. They agreed that they'd buy when Lyle got transferred to a larger place.

Lyle entered the house. No smell of home cooking greeted him. It was 6:30 PM.

There is no amount of training that could prepare members for what Lyle saw today. Once the requested teams, ambulance, and social worker for the little girl arrived, Lyle and Stu returned to Coronach. The investigative officers, two members with the Regina RCMP Major Crimes Unit, relieved Corporal Jennings and Constable Barnes of any primary role in the murder investigation.

Inside, he removed his heavy belt that held a taser, flashlight, revolver, amunition, pepper spray, cuffs, and radio. He laid the belt on the kitchen table.

"Anita, I'm home," Lyle called out. No response. Lyle went to the fridge, grabbed a beer, and sat on a kitchen chair.

Just then a motor stopped outside. The back door opened, and Anita appeared with a bag of Chinese food.

"Some fine food for my favourite cop," she said. Anita placed the food on the kitchen table, went to the fridge, and got a beer for herself. "Pretty hot for April."

"Yeah, I was out in the Big Muddy today and the afternoon sun was beating down on us." He paused, collecting his thoughts.

"Anita, I saw evidence of pure evil today." He told her about his day. The story sent shivers of horror through her body; she shed silent tears for the slain family.

They did not eat right away, preferring to drink more beer in silence, alone with their individual thoughts.

Corporal Lyle Jennings was thirty-seven years old. He was a fifteen-year veteran in the RCMP, originally from Nova Scotia. He had been posted to Coronach, Saskatchewan, a year ago as the officer-in-charge.

Anita grew up in Saskatoon, Saskatchewan. She was twenty-five years old. Twenty-five-year-old city girls with a university degree don't like their lives wasted in nowhere land. Anita was bored. What was there to do in a place with 675 people, one bar, three restaurants, no shops, and miles away from Regina, the only real large city in the south? Her hometown, Saskatoon, had a population 400,000 people; she missed her friends and family and all the amenities available in the city.

The couple was childless. Married three short years ago, she had thought marrying that handsome, broad-shouldered, 6-foot 2-inch Mountie in his red serge was going to be exciting and fun, but it turned out to be far different.

He was on duty a lot. She was alone in their rented home just off Main Street. The town was so small; every home was just off Main Street. She had met a few people. There was a married school teacher who was near her age. But that woman liked life in Coronach. She was originally from around there. Her husband was a SaskPower employee, the major employer in the area. The SaskPower workers and families are close-knit, almost like a large extended family. Anita was married to the local cop. She was an outsider. The two other Mounties were single.

Coronach had depended on the SaskPower Poplar River Plant for power. That's where most of the townspeople had been employed. It was a coal-fired power station that was closed in 2030 on orders from the federal government issued in 2020. The New Green Party (NGP), which held power in Saskatchewan, had supported the closure since 2028.

The plant was located on the banks of the Poplar River. In order to provide cooling water for the plant, the river was damned in the 1970s and 1980s. The plant was once part of SaskPowers' significant coal mining operations in southeast Saskatchewan that accounted for 40 percent of Saskatchewan's energy. The mining operations contributed a great deal to greenhouse gas emissions until the Canadian government ordered them closed.

Near the town of Coronach, lithium had been discovered in saltwater brines that surrounded the Southeast Saskatchewan oil fields. Lithium was used in electric car batteries. Lithium-ion batteries charge faster, last longer, and have a higher power density for more battery life in a lighter package. The NGP, through its Crown corporation, Sask-Power, invested in a battery-making operation in Coronach to create new jobs in the area and stimulate the regional economy. The new operation supplied a world market demand that increased as the making of electric cars worldwide surged tenfold by 2032. Global warming had pushed governments and the car industry into converting vehicle manufacturing from gas- and oil-fueled to electric vehicles.

Anita waited anxiously for Lyle's next transfer. They bickered when she complained. Lyle only cared about promotions and whether a transfer put him in a suitable spot to learn more and if it would be a good mark on his resume. Her griping put him on edge.

He tried to placate her by buying expensive, all-inclusive vacations during the winter months. They often visited her parents in Saskatoon when he got time off. And they'd visited his family in Nova Scotia last summer. But they always had to return to Coronach.

Sometimes he'd say, "If you're so bored, find a job."

When he told her this, she'd think to herself, "What a lunkhead? He's got the brains to know there's no work for her in Coronach." She'd like to scream, "You insensitive bastard!" No, her marriage was not working out like she'd dreamed it would.

Of course, like her dad always told her, "It takes two to tango." Her mom told her to bite her tongue, "After all, he's a hunk, a Mountie."

She had told Lyle before they were married that she would never bear a child. From her perspective, the human race's time on earth was going to end in the next 100 years, either from global warming or atomic bombs. No use raising a child with such a dismal future. He'd broken off with her before their marriage because of that, but he came back, agreeing they wouldn't have children. After they were married though, he asked her if she would change her mind. When she said no, he pouted.

After eating the Chinese food, Lyle went to the living room with another bottle of beer and tequila. Anita sat near him in another chair. They were still silent. She did not wish to interrupt his thinking. Being beside him in silence seemed the right thing to do. Anita felt a caring toward him. She wanted to comfort him. Maybe she could help him with some caressing that might lead to love making.

Lyle lifted the shot glass to his lips and poured its contents into his mouth, then took a chug of beer. He placed his head down on his arms resting across his knees, staring at the floor. When he raised his head, Anita saw tears flow down his cheeks. Silence still. He did not want to speak.

After finishing his drink, he looked up at Anita and said, "There were five bodies, five dead migrants, four shot from close range, execution-like. Never, never, did I imagine something as atrocious as this would happen on my watch."

Anita did not ask any questions. She just let him talk.

"Three of them were teens."

He reached for the bottle of tequila, held it in his hands, and stared straight ahead, trying to decide if he needed another shot and another swig of beer. Lyle put the bottle down. Getting drunk would not make him feel any better.

"I found a young girl alive. She must've strayed in the dark from her family. We have sent her to Regina."

Lyle continued to ramble, telling Anita the people were brown skinned with no identification on them. The people who did this stripped the victims of items that might identify them.

"I have to meet with the investigators and Stu and Fred at the detachment tomorrow morning."

Anita spoke at last. "Will you have access to trauma counselling?"

"Yeah. HQ will send someone down here, but I don't need that shit. I just want whoever did this to be caught. And counselling might look bad on my personnel file. I don't want anything that is detrimental on my file to delay my next promotion."

"Lyle, why would counselling after what you saw be a mark against you?" challenged Anita.

"Because, my dear, needing a shrink makes me look weak and unable to do my job. It's not worth it to have the counselling. Better to just get over it and move on. You want out of here, right? Then don't push it. I'm gonna have a shower and go to bed now," said Lyle.

There was no caressing that led to lovemaking.

THE NEXT MORNING Lyle entered the detachment's meeting room. Stu and Fred Zimmer, his other constable, were already there.

"Good morning, guys. How are you doing?" asked Lyle.

Stu nodded okay, but Lyle could see he had not slept well either.

"Whew," piped in Fred, "what a shit storm. Never thought so much evil existed."

"Well, it does, and it has found its way to our little corner of the world. Stu, HQ will send counselling services down here. We'll be obligated to be receptive for the initial assessment. After that, it will be up to you if you want to continue."

The burly, 40-year-old veteran nodded that he understood.

At that moment, two plain-clothes officers came in. They were Sergeant Dagenais and Corporal Winkler from the Major Crimes Unit.

The two investigators brought the men up to speed.

"The ATV tracks at the scene led north to highway 36. The trail ended there. The killers must have loaded their ATVs onto trucks and headed out from there, either north or south.

We sent the victims' DNA to Interpol authorities to see if the victims could be identified.

Bullet shells found at the scene were fired from high-powered hunting rifles.

The investigators showed pictures of the wrist band to the detachment officers. It was a unique corded leather band about half an inch thick with the words, "Men Rule," carved on it.

Dagenais spoke, "It looks like a hate crime to me. That group the 'Ole Boys' operates around here. They're all about feeling emasculated because of the women's movement. They're also white supremacists."

Lyle spoke, "Sergeant, they've never been more than yahoos blowing hot air in this area. They tell lies about things and hope people are stupid enough to believe them. Their leader is Peter Hamilton, who operates a farm equipment manufacturing business near Willow Bunch. He has been very successful making cultivators, harrows, and tillage. He sells all over Canada and exports a lot to the States. He has three wild boys."

"Thanks, Lyle, he's on our radar. Ten years ago, he was arrested in Ottawa during the Freedom Convoy."

"We've had our disagreements with them," replied Lyle. "Mostly with the boys. We've arrested them on an assortment of charges from DUIs to bullying folks in bars. Stupid is what I'd call them."

The Sergeant looked about the small room. "Lyle, we'll be at the Coronach Hotel for the next while. We'll need this room from time to time."

"For sure, and we'll listen for any news in our community," said Lyle.

6

PETER HAMILTON
WILLOW BUNCH SASKATCHEWAN

The man, in his late 50s, flung the wrench in his hand against his office wall. A crack appeared and plaster dust fell to the floor.

Peter Hamilton is a big fish in this small pond. He is the owner of a business that makes agricultural equipment—seeders, harrows, plows, and cultivators. It is very lucrative business. He had created models of each and started his manufacturing at the turn of the century (2000). He is the largest employer in the Willow Bunch area. That brings him privilege. And he uses that privilege for his own benefit.

He's a bigot; he hates anyone different. Why? Fuck if he even knows why himself. He knows that being a big fish means he can influence others to think his way. His boys are the three people he has influenced most.

"You stupid bastards," he yelled at the three young men standing before him. "Give your heads a shake. Why would you do something like that?"

Lying through his teeth, Donnie, the oldest of the man's boys, answered. It was better that their dad not know exactly what happened. The old man would explode into one of those rages the boys had experienced before. Donnie wanted to avoid his father's wrath.

"Dad, we only started off trying to get them to go back across the border. They were just *spics* sneaking into Saskatchewan, just *spics*. One of them came at Robert, and they struggled causing Robert's rifle to go off, shooting the prick in the gut. The older one, well, he attacked me and got hold of my rifle butt. I pushed him away and fired at him in self-defence. He went down. Two were dead, leaving us with little choice but to shoot the woman and the other boy. They needed to be dead or else we'd be found out. A girl ran off in the dark, fell into a ravine, and broke her neck. They were just *spics*, dad, just *spics*."

Once married, Hamilton's meanness drove his wife and the mother of his three boys away to Calgary. He raised these morons himself, beating them when they deserved it and spoiling them because he could. Punishment and reward, that's how he thought was the best way to control them. They turned out to be loyal to him and hardworking, but they had shit for brains.

Donnie is the oldest at 27, Josh is 25, and the baby Robert is 18. Robert is the weakest link. Hamilton knew he did drugs.

"Did you cover your tracks?" asked Hamilton.

Donnie replied, "Yes, they don't know what direction we went after loading up the ATVs onto the two trucks."

Robert remained quiet. He had not told his brothers about his missing wrist band. It had been only after they left the crime scene that he noticed it was gone.

"Look, boys, you get your stuff together and head for Toronto. Take what money you need. Use the Cadillac XT4. You can contact Merle Jensen through the Ole Boys in Toronto. He'll help you out. We can face-time over the internet. Don't tell anyone what you did here. Am I clear?"

The three boys nodded their heads that they understood.

It was ten years since Peter Hamilton joined a trucker friend and went to Ottawa for the February 2022 Freedom Convoy protests. Then, hundreds of long-haul truckers in their rigs journeyed to Ottawa from different parts of the country to protest Covid-19 mandates and restrictions. They converged on Parliament Hill on January 29, 2022. Thousands of pedestrian protesters joined the truckers.

It took the City of Ottawa by surprise on how well it had been organized and how disruptive the protest was. The protesters blocked city traffic. They harassed many downtown residents. While claiming to be fighting for the rights and freedoms of all Canadians, they stole peace and freedom from the downtown residents. Pressure mounted on Ottawa's mayor and police force, the Ontario Premier, and the Canadian Prime Minister to clear the protesters out of Ottawa. Canadians, including the trucking industry and labour organizations, condemned the protest and demanded removal and arrest of the protestors.

On February 11th, the premier of Ontario declared a state of emergency. On February 14th, the Prime Minister invoked the Emergencies Act. An operation by a combined police/military force broke up the protesters by removing parked vehicles, dismantling blockades, and arresting the organizers and the most disruptive protestors.

While in Ottawa, Hamilton engaged in long talks with far-right extremists who'd joined the fray to promote their hate agenda. It drew Hamilton to a group calling itself the Ole Boys.

The Ole Boys hated government, political correctness, and equal rights except for people like themselves, and showed meanness toward others who disagreed with them. They would eventually turn to violence to achieve their aims.

The Ole Boys originated in New Brunswick. The group had formed in the 1960s to fight New Brunswick bilingualism. Failing to prevent that, they took on more anti-government activism. They protested women and gay rights, gun control, marijuana legalization, acceptance of refugees from non-white nations, seat belt legislation, fishing restrictions, and anything else where they felt the government was being invasive.

Hamilton liked what he heard. Upon his return to southern Saskatchewan, he sought out like-minded men and organized an Ole Boys chapter in his area. In 2022, it had not been difficult. There were many nearby who supported the Convoy and were displeased with the arrest and detention of the Convoy leaders. Hamilton wore his own arrest and charges as a badge of honour. The authorities had subsequently stayed his charges.

For Hamilton, it was not the killing of the *spics* that bothered him; it was that his boys had done it so clumsily. The RCMP would be coming, that's for sure. The Ole Boys would be first on their list of suspects. They'd be coming soon to interview him and his boys. Best they were gone.

Hate had been easy to plant in his boys' hearts. Since they were little, he had been cruel to them. His wife had intervened, so he scared her with the threat of violence until she had no option but to run off. Hamilton threatened her if she ever tried to contact the boys. He got the boys to believe she had run away from being their mother. They hated her. He blamed teachers, police, hospital workers, town workers, just about anybody, if things went wrong. Blaming others was just about the most effective way to teach his boys hate.

THE RCMP KNOCKED at his door at his Willow Bunch home in the early evening. Two plainclothes and a couple of constables drove into his yard in two police cruisers. Electric motors, Hamilton laughed to himself, "They'd never catch the gas-burning XT4."

The investigators asked him if he had any Ole Boys working for him and, if yes, where they could find them.

"Nah, none here. Just hardworking boys who grew up in this area. Because of my business, they are able to remain and raise families in the area," was his response.

The police asked, "Where are your boys?"

"They've run off somewhere. Didn't want to work for me as hard as the others. Thought I'd treat 'em special. No such luck. I told them to piss off. You're no sons of mine, I said to them."

"Mr. Hamilton, we are detaining you on suspicion of a serious crime. You will accompany us to Coronach. You may have counsel meet you at the detachment."

"What the fuck are you charging me with?" Hamilton sputtered.

"Nothing. We can hold you for 24 hours without having to charge you."

7

REBECCA MAHON
REGINA, SASKATCHEWAN

"Saskatchewan's number one radio talk show is pleased to have our Premier with us today," announced host Dean Williams.

"Madame Premier, thank you for taking the time to join us this morning. I know you are so busy these days leading Saskatchewan forward into a new era of economic growth. Please tell us a little about your beginnings."

"Dean, thank you for inviting me. Hello to all your listeners.

Before she responded, her memories went back to Melfort, Saskatchewan. She asked herself, "How did a frail gay person lead the NGP to power?"

She began, "I was born in Melfort, Saskatchewan. My father was a research scientist at the Melfort Research Station. My mother was a schoolteacher at the high school. They encouraged me to learn how to learn from an early age. I thrived in school."

She paused as she recalled when it was that she realized it was girls who attracted her. She was in her early teens. At the time she revealed this to her parents, they responded with love and care. Her mother told her, "Rebecca, be true to yourself. Never wish to be different. Your inner strength will grow as you develop into an adult by thinking positively about yourself, and through your contribution to our society and by showing caring and compassion for others, particularly those most in need. Don't allow others to influence you otherwise."

Rebecca embraced what her mother told her. It helped her when some teens in her high school taunted her about being different. She warned those homophobic teens that she would not put up with their continuing bullshit anti-gay slurs. When they ignored her warning, she went to the school principal and demanded she put a stop to it. The principal held the teens accountable. The slurring against Rebecca stopped. Rebecca learned that an office like the high school principal's held power and, if used rationally and legally, can make a difference for people. That lesson, and others led her determination to seek public office. Holding power and authority would be her way to do good for her community.

Rebecca continued, "After graduating high school, I attended the University of Saskatchewan, where I majored in political science and economics. My grades were good enough to be accepted into graduate school. I earned my Masters in Political Science in 2006.

"I met Sammy Nelson at the university. Most of you know she's my partner and my Chief of Staff. Sammy was studying for her doctorate in Environmental Biology. It was Sammy who helped shape my views about government's responsibility to its people and to its ecological system. My parents taught me about social justice, and respect for everyone and love for my physical surroundings, but it was Sammy who guided me toward environmental activism."

Williams asked, "Madame Premier, voters elected you to the Saskatchewan Legislature as a Saskatoon opposition member of the legislature in 2014, but in 2020, you resigned from the Party. Why?"

"Dean, I became disappointed with the Saskatchewan New Democratic Party's failure to embrace change. I felt necessary to move Saskatchewan economy from dependency on fossil fuels to a green economy. I also felt the Party would not defeat the Saskatchewan Party by fighting issues by pointing them out but not presenting any solutions.

"Listeners may recall in the 2024 election, the issues were doctors fleeing, nurses leaving, lowest wages in Canada, opioid deaths worsening, homeless shelter closings, children's hospitals over capacity and the worst province for domestic abuse. Voters re-elected the Saskatchewan Party because Saskatchewan people felt the New Democratic Party was not up to solving these issues."

Williams commented, "So, your party, the NGP, defeated the Saskatchewan Party in 2028. The Saskatchewan Party had been in power for 21 years. Your party had been only around for 8 years when you beat them at the polls."

"Yes Dean, that's right. We did it by offering a vision of a prosperous, faster growing green economy with higher paying jobs and improved health care, educational services, and the social safety net."

Williams asked, "But don't you think the Saskatchewan Party helped in its own defeat? Many saw the cash payments to the citizens made just prior to the last provincial election as an attempt to buy votes. Inviting Thatcher to the 2022 throne speech was arrogance beyond belief. The public did not agree that a former Saskatchewan politician convicted of murder should be an invited guest. Afterwards, the premier did not apologize for the faux pas right away. *Holy crap*, thought many Saskatchewanians, *the Saskatchewan Party is so out of tune with the values of its people.*

"Then they released the White Paper meant to affirm our constitutional authority over the province's natural resources. That already forms part of the Canadian Constitution. Many in the province viewed it as government pandering to the interests of the powerful fossil fuel industries. Others said it was just a tired group trying to hold onto power, using old time politics of picking a fight with the federal government and trying to have voters believe the Saskatchewan Party was the only party that would defend them against a big, bad, central government. And many Saskatchewan economists pooh-poohed the Saskatchewan Party's environmental cost estimates for federal policies that were being introduced over 12 years."

"Yes, the premier claimed the cost to the province would be $111 billion. I feel the paper divided the Saskatchewan people. There were those who distrusted the federal government and were leery of environmental policies that could hurt Saskatchewan's economic future. And there were those who felt that greenhouse gas emissions left unimpeded would destroy our environment for their children and grandchildren. And there were many sitting on the fence who were unfamiliar with or even interested in the matter.

"The Saskatchewan Party also flirted with selling off some Crown Corporations. But they wouldn't be honest with voters about their intention. The NGP asked voters how would they like these well paying head office jobs for the Crowns to be moved to Toronto or Calgary.

"Remember, the Saskatchewan Party had been ready to introduce small nuclear reactors to generate energy for the province to replace the lost energy resulting from the federal government's mandated closure of the coal mines. Many

Saskatchewan people were sceptical about nuclear reactors. The project had a five-billion-dollar price tag. Would Saskatchewan people appreciate increased energy and power bills? There was also the matter of nuclear waste disposal that worried people. No one wants that dumped in their back yard."

Williams countered, "But your government has invested heavily in nuclear fusion. It has been nearly as expensive as the reactors."

"Yes, we have. Unlike reactors that break an atom up and create waste, referred to as fission, we've invested in atom fusion that happens when two or more atoms are fused into one, larger one. Unlike nuclear fission, it doesn't generate long lasting radioactive waste. After initial investments, the cost of producing sustainable electricity is far less expensive than a reactor. We've kept the cost of electricity in Saskatchewan relatively low for consumers. It's great pricing for our manufacturers, making them very competitive worldwide."

Williams smiled, "Madame Premier, you were very persuasive. You defeated them by offering an alternative. Please tell us about that."

"Sure. Recall our slogan in the 2028 election was *It's our Future*. We offered to grow a new sustainable economy without continuing to harm the environment through the production of energy from fossil fuels. We told voters we would improve the lives of all Saskatchewan people by sharing the enormous opportunities and potential wealth from a cleaner economy. This green, cleaner economy is a low-carbon, resource efficient, and socially inclusive. We were honest that we'd run deficits to pay for the change, but in a few years our investments would pay for state-of-the-art medical care, the best education system possible, and an improved safety net for all."

Williams asked, "Saskatchewan still has problems with domestic abuse and homelessness. You've not delivered on those issues. Why?"

"I am disappointed we've not made substantial inroads on domestic abuse in the province. We've increased funding for awareness programs and safe houses. Our province is the first in Canada to provide transitional allowances for persons who've left abusive domestic relationships. This enhanced social assistance for the abused is provided along with funding for employment readiness assessment, counselling, and relocation help. We are still working to find better approaches.

"As for homelessness, our phenomenal economic growth has attracted so many workers from within Canada and immigrants to fill our labour needs. Builders and developers are finding it difficult to find construction workers to build new housing to keep up with our population growth. We are recruiting construction workers and offering bonuses like relocation allowances and tax incentives to attract tradesman. Adequate housing is one of our biggest challenge. Since 2022, our population has gone from 1.2 million to 1.7 million."

Williams commented, "Yes, our Province is undergoing a remarkable transformation. Your government's approval rating is at 63 percent; most people like what's happening."

Rebecca Mahon chortled, "We'll accept credit, of course. That's part of politics. But, our opportunity to make the change is due to our riches in natural resources that are in demand worldwide and are integral to the efforts to combat climate change."

Williams asked, "Specifically lithium?"

"You're right, Dean. The jewel in Saskatchewan's resources is lithium. Lithium, with public and private investment, has become a source of great export revenue for Saskatchewan. Western countries, particularly western Europe, Japan, and South Korea, are leery of being dependent on Afghanistan, Russia, and China for the lithium needed for electric car batteries and cleaner powered appliances. So they turned to Saskatchewan. But this province is more than just exporting lithium. Where lithium is being mined, electric car battery manufacturing is happening nearby.

"Public and private investment partnerships make this possible. Workers once employed in the fossil fuels industries have found good-paying jobs in lithium mining and battery production."

Williams said, "Thank you, Madame Premier. I hope you can return soon. Do you have any parting words for our listeners that foretell our Province's future?"

Rebecca Mahon responded, "Robert Kennedy once said, *'Progress is a pleasant word. But change is its motivator. And change has its enemies.'*

"Political power is a house of cards. Despite a booming economy and improved public services, there are people wanting to bring the house crashing down. We have detractors skulking about, looking for reasons to discredit our initiatives. Some gas and oil interests want to turn the clock back. There are far-right groups who hate the idea of a gay premier. There are workers whose jobs became redundant who refuse retraining opportunities. And the list goes on. It's my job to work to reach out to them and show them the future can be as good for them as others."

Williams stated, "Madame Premier, you sound more like a luminary than a politician."

Mahon responded, "I'd prefer to be known as a unifier. I coax people and convince them there's something in it for them. We provide tax credits, subsidies, automobile buybacks, and grants to promote our green economy agenda. We've borrowed to do this, but our government revenues are increasing, allowing us to pay down debt.

"My government has also respected First Nations and Métis rights in our policies and legislation. For example, the only oil and gas allowed to be produced by oil companies is from leased treaty land.

"Our desire to maintain ownership over SaskPower and SaskEnergy has been important in the change from fossil fuels to cleaner energy sources. These entities have showed leadership, employee expertise, organization, networks, and infrastructure to convert to cleaner energy sources."

∼

AFTERWARDS, in her car, she mentally reviewed the NGP's five fundamental principles to ensure that she had not wandered from them during her radio interview.

Tomorrow is today. Nothing will exist if action doesn't start now. Soon enough, it might be all over. Sammy emphasized this as the most important principle. For far too long, people have seen the greenhouse gas emission issue as something too difficult to address today. Thinking another day will produce solutions, people avoided the problem for as long as possible.

Everyone is a winner. Individuals, small businesses, and communities affected by change will receive transition grants to offset their losses. Sammy understood that deniers of climate change will refuse to accept the truth about something that is happening in their life. She also predicted that enormous sums of dark money will come into the province to discredit the NGP. It will come from self-interested big oil and gas companies and companies that use oil as a raw material in their products, like plastics, bubble gum, fertilizers, chemical products, medicine, gel capsules, and paints. But she knew that communicating that change was necessary and that everyone will benefit was well worth the effort.

Champions are needed now. Who will fan out over the province talking about the facts, even with those who disagree? To speak at the grocery store, in church, at picnics, trade shows, and parties, telling everyone about the reality of the climate crisis. To tell people that the transition to a green economy will create thousands of well-paying and safe jobs while improving peoples' health.

Partnership of private and public investments. These partnerships lead to economic activities in building infrastructure and assets that reduce carbon emissions and pollution; enhance energy, resource efficiency, and biodiversity; and prevent damage to ecosystems.

Fairness in a green society. Every human being deserves political, economic and social rights and opportunities.

~

Sammy Nelson, Mahon's Chief of Staff, is standing in Rebecca's office when she arrives back from the radio studio. Sammy is pacing with a document in her hands.

"What's up, Sammy?" asked Rebecca.

"There has been a mass murder in the Big Muddy. This is a briefing note from Justice. Five in a family of Hispanics who crossed our border near Coronach. There is one young girl who survived. She is with child protection now."

"Oh my God, who could have done this? That poor family and that little girl who survived, what will this do to her?" asked a heartsick Rebecca.

Sammy replied, more worried about the right messaging than the tragedy, "You may recall, you may not, but in the late 20th century, MacLean's Magazine once had an article titled *Saskatchewan is the Alabama of the North*. We don't want that type of narrative coming out of this. Rebecca, you need to release a media statement that condemns what has happened, and that everything is being done to track down those brutal murderers."

Mahon nodded her agreement, "Sammy, arrange for a draft to be prepared at once. We'll get ahead of it. And please inform the senior RCMP officer to keep me abreast of their investigation."

8

WALKER INTERVIEWS WONG
REGINA, SASKATCHEWAN

Walker met Wong at the door of the studio. They shook hands. Walker pointed his guest to a chair facing the microphone at the table, "Please sit."

"Is it Professor or Doctor?" asked Walker.

"If you promise me that you'll go easy on me, you can call me Peter, and I hope I can call you Allan. For the podcast, please refer to me as Dr. Wong."

"Works for me," answered Walker. "I assume you know all about podcasts. Been around now for 20 years."

"Sure, I'm familiar. I've read you have one of the largest followings in the world. You must have become a very wealthy man."

Walker pondered that comment. He thought most people must think he was getting rich from his growing fan base. But no, he was donating his ad profits to immigrant assistance programs, climate change prevention, and the USA organization working against the right-wing extremists. He needed no money outside of the modest salary he took.

"It's lucrative, for sure, but I operate on a salary and gift the rest away."

"Oh, you've a cause. A young man with a cause. I like you already. Well, I'm glad I'm being interviewed by a righteous man with righteous causes," said Wong.

Walker smiled. He liked this handsome older man.

"I also interview people who disagree with me. It's often distasteful, but I believe I expose to my audience how twisted they are. Greed is their motivator. They're paid well by people who benefit from their lies. They peddle misinformation using their bogus science or conspiracy theories, and flaunt educational degrees to support their lies. Pure evil, pure evil, and my listeners learn that."

"Peter, I'm a great admirer of your writings on the dangers of global warming. Can we begin now? I'll ask for some very basic climate change fundamentals in our first half-hour podcast. Most people are up on this stuff, especially younger kids, but I like to do it this way so future episodes are based on the building blocks. Is that okay with you?"

Wong nodded his agreement.

Walker adjusted the microphones, set the computer for sound proofing and noise control, and adjusted the recording of the conversation.

After Walker ran the introductions and ads, he introduced Wong with an emphasis on his guest's knowledge of climate change.

"Dr. Wong, welcome. It's an honour to have you on my podcast."

"You're welcome, Mr. Walker. I'm happy to be here."

"Dr. Wong, I introduced you as an authority on climate change. For my audience, tell me what is the difference between climate change and global warming?"

Wong replied, "People use the terms interchangeably in discussing the issues. Greenhouse gas emission causes climate change, and the climate change is why the planet is warming,"

"Doctor Wong, what is greenhouse gas emission?"

Wong answered, "Think of a greenhouse. Sunlight comes into the greenhouse, and plants and soil absorb it. The greenhouse windows ensure the warmer air is retained. The inside of the greenhouse warms up."

Wong paused, cleared his throat, and then continued.

"During the day, the sun shines through the earth's atmosphere, warming the earth's surface. At night, the earth's surface cools, releasing heat back into the air. Greenhouse gases in the earth's atmosphere trap heat like a blanket wrapped around the earth. Without these greenhouse gases, it would be too cold to have life on the planet. Greenhouse gases are composed mostly of carbon dioxide.

"But human use of fossil fuels like coal and oil is putting too much carbon dioxide into our atmosphere. Our planet is heating because too much heat is being trapped."

Wong paused again, hoping the listeners would understand his explanation when the podcast came out.

"Up until about 1850, before the Industrial Age started mass production, earth had been in a natural balance where greenhouse gas emissions warmed the earth and enough heat escaped into space to avoid global warming. Mass production required using fossil fuels to generate energy for factories.

"Mass production resulted in growing prosperity and rising population. Cheap energy has been the heart of human progress and wellbeing. Our desire for more stable food and water supplies, increased comfort and pleasures, and individual prosperity has created a reliance on fossil fuels.

"Mr. Walker, if you ask me what our single biggest challenge is in saving our planet, I will tell you it's the need to reprogram ourselves. God naturally wired us to fear change. Our leaders must prepare us by explaining the urgency to change, present a positive vision of our future, and provide an outline of the journey ahead. Our ancestors needed to move around to search for food, water, and shelter. If they hadn't, it could've led to their demise. It would've been the leader of the pack who guided his followers to a new location that had the essential resources.

"Our planet's temperature rose .08 C between 1854 and 1981. The rate of warming between 1981 and 2021 increased by .18 C. It rose again by 1.7 C between 2021 and 2032. That number is alarming.

"This warming acceleration is moving our planet toward a point of no return. By the year 2100, our planet may be too hot for humans to live as we do today. Domes with piped-in fresh air may have to be built to house humans and animals and to grow food. Water supplies on earth may no longer exist if it is being used to generate energy from fossil fuels. Of course, a heated earth means far less annual rainfall. Some scientist predict this could happen by 2040. Space travel to discover alternative sources of water may be our only alternative unless we stop using fossil fuels."

Like a pastor giving a Sunday sermon, Wong stopped speaking for effect and then started in a louder voice, "Don't you think it would be easier if our global leadership and you, our citizens, took this seriously now, banned fossil fuels, and moved more quickly to cleaner energy sources? It's your children and grandchildren whose lives are being held in the balance."

When time was up, Walker ran more ads, then asked, "Dr. Wong, what will you speak about on our next podcast?"

"Mr. Walker, I wish to speak about destructive deforestation."

"And so it will be. Folks, please email or message me with your comments and any questions you want Dr. Wong to answer."

After the recorder was turned off, Walker turned to his guest, "Thank you, Peter. I think that went well. I'll be busy this afternoon editing it for tonight's release, but my partner Judy and I would like you to join us for dinner this evening at around 7 PM. What do you say?"

"Absolutely, I'd be happy to join you," replied Wong.

Walker provided him an address.

∽

Near 7 PM, a quiet electric taxi pulled up on Angus Street in front of a 1920s three-story red brick home with a screened-in porch at the front. Wong paid the driver, walked up to the porch door, and rang the bell. An attractive thirty plus woman in blue jeans and a bright red blouse opened the front door, inviting him in.

"Dr. Wong, I assume?" greeted the woman.

"That'd be me," he replied with a generous smile. "And I assume you are Allan's lady friend." The sweet aroma of weed wafted from inside as Wong handed a bottle of red wine and flowers to the woman.

"Oh, aren't you kind? Yes, I'm Judy. Please come in. Allan will be out in a minute. We own the house but live only on this floor. We rent out rooms on the second and third floor to newcomers to Canada."

"Peter, please come into the sitting room," called Allan. "What would you like to drink? I've whiskey and bourbon."

"Don't suppose you have Five Star Whiskey?"

Allan looked puzzled.

"Just joshing with you. Back in the 60s my dad and his friends passed a lot of time drinking Five Star Whiskey and gambling. I don't think it's made anymore. Bourbon will be fine."

Walker left and returned with only one drink.

"Hmm, you're not joining me?" asked Wong.

"No," responded Walker. "I fought demons from drinking years ago. I lost family and jobs and self-respect for it. I'll smoke a joint instead. Canada legalized pot 15 years ago."

Wong looked at him, took a sip of the bourbon, and said, "Demons have played havoc with me as well. Not booze. I'm pretty sure you know about my gambling."

"I do my research, Peter, and knew we were a pair of addicts. Jenny's cooking up a storm, so once your drink is done, we'll sit in the dining room and enjoy good food and conversation."

"Sounds good to me. And it smells delicious!"

At the dining room table, Wong asked Judy, "So Judy, besides being a fabulous cook, what else do you do?"

"You're a charmer, Peter. I work for a community-based, non-profit settlement service for immigrants called Regina Welcomes You. Our funding comes from the federal and provincial governments as well as our own fundraising," she replied.

"Interesting, very interesting indeed. Where are your immigrants coming from?" asked Peter.

"Well, we have refugees arriving from places in southeast Africa. Wars and persistent drought have forced their migration. Millions are dying there. The ones who are able to escape to temporary refugee camps in Europe are relocated to countries willing and able to accept them, like Canada. The immigrants are moved to localities across Canada. Regina Welcomes You and other non-profit immigration settlement services play a pivotal role in safely settling them in their communities.

"We also continue to have refugees from eastern Europe as Russian continues its aggression to re-establish control over its former Soviet bloc nations. As you know, that war has been going on since 2022. Millions of eastern Europeans, mostly Ukrainians and Russians, have been driven from their homeland. Many are making their way to Saskatchewan."

Wong shifted in his chair and said, "Yes, sad, and to think that when Putin died in 2025, the West thought new Russian leadership would change things. But no, the new leadership threatens nuclear war if the West intervenes, and the American President Harrison Petry informs NATO that the US won't intervene because it has little interest in Europe and its problems. There is a real lack of moral and compassionate leadership in the United States under Petry's presidency. That war might continue for many years unless the most powerful nation on the planet intervenes."

Judy continued, "Yes, you're bang on. People have been driven from their homes since the beginning of time. Fortunately, history's great migration has often brought migrants to better lives in new places. Saskatchewan is a wonderful place for people who've never had freedom. There's an ample supply of clean water and an abundance of food in a land with vast open spaces and urban centres that are just big enough but not too big.

"Saskatchewan immigration has grown annually from 3,700 in the year 2020 to 30,000 in 2030. Regina's share of that is about 8,000 new Canadian residents."

Wong smiled at Judy, "You are a most wonderful promoter of this province. I'm an immigrant. Regrettably, when my father came to Canada, Saskatchewan was not as welcoming to him as it would be today. And, when I came and joined him after my mother died in China, he had to pay a tax when I entered Canada. Chinese people were the only immigrants required to pay that tax. I'm very pleased to hear that there are people like you and organizations like Regina Welcomes You."

"Peter, I'm so sorry. I am familiar with that draconian measure. So, you've been living in England for many years now? Are you familiar with the American migration to Canada?"

"Judy, I've read a little, but not a lot."

"America's own citizens are coming to Canada. It's just beginning. Americans are leaving to escape far-right extremism, lawlessness, a cascading automatic weapons crisis, drought, destructive storms, flooding, forest fires, water shortages, and significant job losses in southern states all impacted by global warming. American immigrants are our fastest growing newcomers to Saskatchewan."

Wong replied, "I've read about this migration in an article published by the Intergovernmental Panel on Climate Change (IPCC)."

Allan asked, "Peter, tell me about that organization."

"The IPCC researches and publishes information on climate change. They've said this unimaginable migration north from what is the richest country on earth is just the beginning of a global migration from the hot Southern Hemisphere to the North."

Wong wiggled his nose in disgust and the corners of his mouth turned down as he expressed his disdain for the United States.

"Back in the summer of 2023, the United States Democratic-controlled Congress introduced a far-reaching bipartisan clean energy package that would've invested 369 billion into combating global warming. However, the package never passed in the Republican-controlled Senate.

"Then Petry defeated Biden in 2024 and that ended hopes that the United States would be a global leader against climate change. No one ever thought someone might be worse than Trump. Petry has proven them wrong."

Wong took a sip of wine, then pivoted by asking his hosts, "So, how did you two meet?"

Walker smiled, "Judy came to my studio to be interviewed for a podcast on immigration. I was smitten right away."

"Judy, where are you from?" asked Wong.

"Born, educated and working in good ole Regina. Like you, my undergraduate degree is from the University of Regina."

"Fellow alumnus. And, Allan, what's your background?" asked Wong.

Walker shifted, then responded. "Nah, its an unpleasant history with booze. I don't wish to speak about my past."

∼

Wong got back to his place around 11 PM. It had been a splendid evening. Now he had one more task before he could go to bed.

He opened his laptop. Then he clicked on the face-to-face icon. The man in Washington answered.

"Tell me what you have," ordered the unpleasant man.

"I'm not sure it's him."

"Fuck you, you got a photo."

"I know, but they took it in 2020. It's been twelve years since then. We met in his studio and just did our interview. I'll learn more from him next time," said Wong.

"Okay, I'll hold the dogs back for now. But remember, if you don't deliver, I'll set them on you."

"I understand," replied Wong.

After the call, Wong told himself, if I tell him now, I do not solve my dilemma. Wong didn't want to be party to a murder, but he didn't want to die either. That's the dilemma. Better to stall and see if he could wiggle out of this corner.

9

BILL LARSEN
WASHINGTON DC

The call displeased the man. Wong was stalling. Larsen had been bullying people far too long not to know when someone was reluctant to do the task assigned to him. But he knew he had Wong by the balls. One word from him to the men Wong owed money to would set Wong's execution in motion. For now, he'd cut Wong some slack. Allan Walker was his man. And he was not going anywhere.

Bill Larsen was a political consultant and lobbyist for all things ultraconservative and for all things that served his self-interest. By promoting false narratives and conspiracy theories, he helped far-right conservative candidates win local, state, and federal elections. He received legal and illegal earnings for his efforts, making him a very wealthy man. And, for most of his 79 years, he had stayed off the radar of police authorities and the media. That was until that drunken CNN reporter started poking his nose into his affairs.

That man was Dan Weber. Larsen was certain that Walker is Weber. Weber is the man who informed America about how Larsen had helped his close friend Harrison Petry win the 2024 presidential election. It was Larsen's imaginative conspiracy theories about Joe Biden, the incumbent Democrat President, that dominated the debates during the 2024 presidential election.

Larsen smiled to himself. His best conspiracy was how Biden, the President of the United States, had approved experimenting with Covid as a bio-warfare weapon and how it leaked from a military lab causing a new outbreak in 2023. Three in ten Americans believed that was true. From there, Larsen created many other conspiracies, destroying the incumbent's re-election chances.

And Larsen created falsehoods that Petry promoted from his huge ultraconservative platform. Among them, Petry espoused lies about government initiatives to fight global warming and gun control. He told Americans that the Democrats wanted gun control so that they could suppress the political rights and civil liberties of individuals. He promoted the conspiracy theory that scientists were manipulating climate data just to have their environmental agenda move forward. Petry won the 2024 election.

Weber became a menace, a nuisance, and a skillful adversary. The man could dig up dirt. During the 2024 election campaign, CNN broadcast Larsen's name in connection with a lobbying scandal. The FBI opened up a file. Soon, he was indicted on federal charges for illegal lobbying for foreign governments and for not reporting lobby earnings from those foreign governments on his tax returns. A federal judge sentenced him to forty months in jail.

After Petry became President, Larsen received a presidential pardon but not before he had spent one year behind bars in a federal penitentiary.

With bitterness and a hunger for revenge, Larsen had been using his wealth to find the bastard responsible for his humiliation. He influenced the President to have the Justice Department use photo matching technology to find a man named Allan Walker living in Regina, Saskatchewan, who was a lookalike match to Weber.

Larsen thought Weber was an imbecile. CNN had fired the man after a drunken episode that saw him appear during Candace Harris's Prime Time News on CNN and slur his words, then mutter 'fuck,' and drop his mic and walk away. Three hundred thousand viewers watched this. Then Fox News and MSNBC replayed it repeatedly to many more viewers. It hurt CNN's image as the leader in world news. Weber's wife of fifteen years had divorced him because of his drinking and got a court order banning him from seeing his small daughter.

Larsen, a teetotaler, looked down on Weber. *A weak man*, he thought. *How could such a weak fuck have caused so much trouble for such an able man as himself?*

As soon as he found the lookalike in Regina and learned about the man's podcasts, he listened to them. This man named Walker was spewing liberal bullshit on immigration, gun control, voters' disenfranchisement, abortion, and climate change. The lookalike sounded like Weber. And like Weber, he was a fucking menace to Larsen and the ultraconservatives. Everything Walker was telling his audience was contrary to Larsen's interests. At his age, he didn't give a rat's ass about the earth warming. He was not a stupid man. But what did he care? He was in his 70s; he had one child in her late forties who had no children. It was in his financial interest to disavow global warnings. Fuck mankind!

Larsen conceived his evil plan to exact revenge. The first step was to confirm that Walker was Weber. Next, he needed a vulnerable, well-known man, someone he could manipulate. He had read Time magazine's article about the famous climate change scientist leaving Oxford to return to his roots in Regina, Saskatchewan. He sent an investigator to London to look into the scientist. The report came back. Wong had a 5-million-dollar problem. That's when Larsen decided that there was a win for him and a win for Wong. Wong was his man to confirm Walker was Weber. After confirmation, he'd hire some local Saskatchewan yahoo to finish the job.

The investigator approached Wong in England and encouraged the scientist to change his flight plans to include a stopover in Washington. He left Wong little choice but to comply.

10

PRESIDENT HARRISON PETRY
OTTAWA, ONTARIO

The Prime Minister of Canada's aide-de-camp knocked on her door.

"Yes Julian, come in," said the Prime Minister.

"Madam Prime Minister, the President of the United States is on line."

Pauline Gervais made a yikes facial expression in jest. Julian smiled at his boss.

"Put him through," said the Prime Minister.

"Hello, Mr. President, this is a pleasant surprise."

"Well, yes, but it's not on a pleasant matter. I've a beef to discuss with you, Pauline."

The Prime Minister thought that this loud buffoon was calling her by her first name as a show of his superiority. She'd call him by his first name. Tit for tat, screw the high road. He was a sexist. She thought of the Philippine mythical creature, the Manananggal, at that moment. The Manananggal with its kite-shaped wings was the same shape as the bleached blond hair on Petry's head. And like Petry, it was a man-eating and blood-sucking creature.

"Oh Harrison, what is on your mind?"

"Liberal news stations, newspapers, and social media are all making out that the death of those four in Sask-chewan, or whatever it's called, resulted from my administration's policies on climate change, gun control, the economy, immigration, or just about any issue the liberal pricks can think of."

The Prime Minister paused as the thought passed through her mind that this man had no policies on anything. He stood for nothing but self-interest and demagoguery.

"Such a tragedy. The family must have been seeking a more secure life in Canada."

"Maybe," his voice becoming belligerent, "you should tighten up your border patrol."

"Come on, Harrison, these poor migrants wouldn't have entered Canada if your borders hadn't been so easy to breech for them to have gotten into your country. They passed through the United States first." 'Gotcha,' she mused.

"Look, don't you get smart with me," responded an angry Petry.

"I'm not, Harrison. I'm telling you how it is. So, is your call about the poor murdered family, or is it about how your border control policies are failing?"

There was a pause, as if Petry were having a problem focusing on what he wanted.

Finally he sputtered hotly, "You might tell me about the investigation."

"Well, Mr. President, we've learned they were a family of six who'd travelled from Central America, crossed your border, and continued north. It was an American Christian organization that aided them in travelling across your country and sneaking into Canada."

"Come on, Pauline, I couldn't give a shit about them and their situation. I'm going to tell folks down here they were drug smugglers. That's my narrative, and I expect your support for that."

"Mr. President, absolutely not!"

"Pauline, you've got a country that depends on us for your security. You're indebted to us. You just can't say no when we come asking."

"Mr. President, Harrison, our country is indebted to the American people, not to you. And, your country has come to ours in times of need. It's not a one-way street. I will report to the Canadian people the truth about what happened."

The Prime Minister heard a click on the other end. The buffoon had hung up on her.

She was about to tell him that the RCMP think an extremist Ole Boy chapter in Saskatchewan was behind the murders. The investigation was ongoing. When she had more, she would let him know. Now she thought, *Fuck him.*

Julian appeared at her door, "Madam Prime Minister, the German Chancellor wishes to speak to you."

Gervais told Julian to put the call through.

The two leaders spoke about Germany's energy needs. Germany had stopped receiving gas and oil from Russia by 2023. Western European countries needed to find alternative energy sources because they had sided with former Soviet Bloc countries in their struggle to thwart Russia's efforts to bring them back under Russian control. The western European countries boycotted Russia from any trade of goods and services. Canada supplied these countries with ammonia gas as an energy source to help them with their needs.

Wind turbines were first built in Newfoundland to produce green hydrogen, which was then used to produce ammonia gas. Ammonia gas, one part nitrogen and three parts hydrogen, was being shipped to Europe to be used to generate power. The project attracted billions in private and public investments. Western European countries lined up to buy the product. The gas was shipped in canisters on ocean freighters to western Europe. Soon, Saskatchewan and Alberta wind turbines would be producing the same hydrogen for ammonia gas.

It had been such a simple idea. The wind turbines produced the electricity required to split water into hydrogen and oxygen. This process was called electrolyzer. They produced electricity with no greenhouse gas emissions.

Germany is Canada's biggest importer of the ammonia gas. That's why the Chancellor was calling. She wanted to find out the status of Canada's efforts to expand green hydrogen production in Saskatchewan and Alberta. Germany wanted to increase its orders.

Prime Minister Gervais informed the Chancellor that the new wind turbines in both provinces would be turned on by the summer of this year. She assured the Chancellor that the German people would have ample heat this winter.

11

MARK JACKSON
CHEYENNE, WYOMING

Jose Kirk was saying goodbye to his brother in Albuquerque.

Last night, he told his younger brother, Raoul, "I've got a job in Regina. We're not entering Canada broke. With the sale of our home and business equipment, we have $300,000. And our money's worth more in Canadian dollars. We'll be fine."

During the evening, the men and their wives talked a lot. Usually, Freda got them talking about some news she'd read online. The others did not keep abreast of what was happening. But they loved to be an expert on whatever she got them talking about. It's called the Dunning-Kruger effect, where people overestimate their ability or knowledge.

That night, they talked about the rising number of migrants from the Caribbean, and Central and South America attempting to enter the southern border of the United States.

They were coming from Peru, Nicaragua, Haiti, Venezuela, and Columbia. Migrants were taking greater risks. They were crossing the hot ranch lands of Texas with children in tow. Many did not have sufficient drinking water. Others were attempting to cross the tumultuous Rio Grande and drowning. For American authorities, it was taking months to identify the bodies and return them to families in their homeland. Due to the frosty relationships between the US and some of those nations, it was difficult and sometimes impossible to get identifying information.

Raoul and his wife said, "Why don't they just get in line?"

Freda answered, "There's no line for these people. They're disadvantaged in their homeland; that's why they flee. Our present government only wants highly skilled people to immigrate. Petry and his cronies are discreet about it, but white immigrants with skills are being fast tracked into the United States from eastern Europe. They are the displaced people from the war-torn regions."

"They should stay where they're from. What could be so bad? President Petry is the only politician who has it right. Make it hard on them to get across the border and, if they sneak and get caught, put them in unpleasant detention facilities until we deport them. Word will get back to where they came from that they're not welcome," said Raoul.

Jose could not hold his tongue. "Raoul, mom was an illegal until President Obama granted amnesty. Freda is an illegal.

Petry is a racist. How can you think that way? You're brainwashed by what you hear at your Chamber of Commerce. These illegals work hard, stay out of trouble and don't cost taxpayers anything. One incident where an illegal commits a violent crime, and it's presented by the conservatives as if they're responsible for every violent crime. Think about it."

Raoul's wife was white. Her name was Jenny. She piped in about something she'd just seen that day on daytime TV. That's what she watched.

"This place you're going to, Saskatchewan, there was a mass murder of a family from Central America. Five dead, parents and three children shot in cold blood. Freda, you missed that?"

"I did, Jenny. Oh my God, that's where we're going, or were," she looked in horror at Jose.

Jose soothed her, "Freda, we are entering with all the papers, making it legal. I've got a job. There's a house waiting for us. And there are red necks everywhere. Tonight, when you're on your tablet, check how many of these situations occur," pleaded Jose. If Freda no longer wanted to go, they wouldn't be going.

∼

THE NEXT MORNING, Freda reported she'd found no similar events like those murders in Saskatchewan's modern history.

Raoul looked at his older brother. He was not joining him. He owned "The Albuquerque Airbrush Vehicle Painting" business, and drought was not affecting them. He and Jenny think Jose and Freda are overreacting. They had asked each other, "Who in their right mind would move up to wherever it is they are going?"

"Good luck, bro," said Raoul

They hugged farewell, and Jose got into their vehicle. He continued their drive north. It was 7 AM. Unlike yesterday's difficult driving through smoke and falling ash from the forest fires, it was a clear day. Yesterday, there had been gusty and erratic winds; today it was calm.

Jose wanted to reach Denver by midafternoon. Traffic on the I25, which cuts through the downtown, is very heavy between 4 PM and 7 PM. It's an hour's drive through the city when the highway isn't busy. It's two hours during the peak traffic hours.

From Denver, they will drive another 2 hours to Cheyenne, where they will stop for the evening.

From Albuquerque, the driving had been easy. But from Santa Fe to the Raton Pass, a cross wind blew embers across the highway. Smoked filled the air. There were fires in the Santa Fe National Forest. Signs on the highway advised motorists not to stop. The Kirks could see fire in the distance to the west of them. The smoke subsided when they drove through the Raton Pass that cut through the Sangre de

Cristos Mountains. The Pass took them from New Mexico into Colorado.

They stopped at a rest stop just inside of Colorado where Jose filled up with gas. The two children took Charlie on a leash to the dog park area for him to do his business. It was 10:45 AM. The weather was cooler here. Freda and Jose had some coffee. When the children returned with Charlie, they had a beverage and a snack. After their pit stop, the Dodge Durango pulled out of the rest area, and turned north on the I25 heading for Denver.

Five hours later, past Denver, they stopped at a Chevron Filling Station to fill up the gas tank. The children took Charlie for a walk while Jose pumped the gas and Freda went to the restroom.

Suddenly, Manuel and Victoria came running toward Jose screaming, "Charlie has run off after jack rabbits!"

Jose completed filling up with gas and went behind the building where Charlie had run off to look for him. The landscape was semi-desert.

Jose called, "Charlie, Charlie, come here, boy."

From his right, a large black man appeared with Charlie on his leash. "Is this Charlie?" he asked with a bright smile that showed sparkling white teeth.

"Oh, yes, thank you so much. I'm so grateful; he's part of our family. Thank you so much," Jose repeated.

The black man replied, "You're welcome. He's a big, friendly boy, isn't he?"

"You bet," smiled Jose.

The man turned Charlie's leash over to Jose. The two men shook hands and wished each other safe travels.

Jose loaded Charlie into the Durango where he received some relieved hugs and friendly scolding from the children. They set off again.

They passed Fort Collins and reached the Wyoming border in good time. The wind's strength had picked up after Fort Collins. Jose needed to hold tight to the steering wheel to prevent the Durango and the U-Haul from veering into the ditch. He was glad when he saw the sign telling him he was approaching Cheyenne.

He pulled his unit into the Cheyenne Walmart situated just off the I25. Walmart allowed motor homes and freight trucks to park overnight in their parking lots. They discouraged all other vehicles. Jose had to find a discreet spot to park overnight.

Jose drove around the parking lot looking for a spot that would block his Durango and U-Haul from sight. He discovered just the place in the southeast corner near the back corner of the parking lot. There were two long motorhomes parked parallel to each other, with about 20 yards between them. Jose maneuvered his unit into that space.

The children got out and ran across the parking lot with their mother to use the store's restroom and purchase a few things. Jose walked Charlie. When he returned to the Durango, he found a small electric vehicle parked in behind their U-Haul between the motor homes.

A man got out of the car. He reached down and touched his toes, then let his arms rest loosely by his sides and shook them, and then stretched his neck. It was the big black man from the Chevron Station.

"Mandy, please get out of the car and stretch out," he called to his passenger.

"Howdy, mister," called out Jose. "Here to check on Charlie?"

"And howdy to you," chuckled the man. "My name is Mark Jackson, and you are?"

"Jose...Jose Kirk," replied Jose.

"Jose, I hope you don't mind us hiding out with you?" said Jackson.

"Of course not," said Jose.

Jackson pointed to his passenger. "This here is Mandy, my daughter."

As Mandy was stepping out of the car, Jose nodded her way, acknowledging the introduction. Freda and the children showed up, and Jose introduced them to the Jacksons.

Freda asked, "Are you up for some sandwiches and pie? We've got lots to share."

"Gee, that's awfully kind of you. Sure, we would be pleased to join you," said Jackson.

After eating, Jose told Jackson, "I'm going to get the kids settled in the car for the night, then maybe we can talk some more."

"I'm going to settle in too, Jose. Nice meeting you, Mr. Jackson," piped in Freda.

"Likewise," answered Jackson. "I'm going to take Mandy to the Walmart restroom then come back. See you then."

When Jackson and Mandy returned, she went to their car to sleep. Jackson joined Kirk. The two men sipped on a bottle of Jose's tequila and talked.

"You're the Mark Jackson, aren't you? The Mark Jackson from 20 years ago? The football guy?" asked Jose.

"That'd be me," the big man replied.

"You're the greatest rookie running back in the history of the National Football League," said Jose.

"There are many other backs who'd contend that they were, but people say numbers don't lie. Anyhow, it matters little. When I tore my meniscus in the playoffs and it didn't heal right, my career turned out to be only that one year. Boy, the money for a new contract was only weeks away.

My agent told me an extension was going to make me rich."

"I know my story is not as illustrious, but I was on the brink of greater wealth too." Jose then told Jackson why he was on the road.

"Jose, my new friend, you worked so hard for what you had. It seemed to be more about luck in my situation. I was lucky to be born with a natural talent. Sure, I worked hard, went to college on a scholarship, stayed out of trouble, and was drafted by the NFL. And then bad luck took away everything I thought I was gonna have. Bad luck sticks to me like glue."

"So, Mark, where are you heading?" asked Jose.

"Same place you are, except I don't have a job to go to. And I've no papers to enter Canada. I was coaching high school ball in Denver, but I quit."

"Why, sounds like a good gig, good money and up your alley."

Mark hesitated. The tequila warmed him up to Jose. He pondered telling this man—he had just meant that bad luck comes in bunches for some men? Decision time—does moving on mean never speaking about it again? Is that even possible? *He* thought, *You know, I've got a good feeling about this guy. We are going to see more of each other in the future. Might as well tell him. At least I'll know how I feel about telling it to another person.*

"Have you heard of the Haney High School shootings in Denver? There were thirty-one students and four staff members killed by a fellow student. The boy entered through the front door of the school with an automatic rifle and a hand gun and went to the auditorium where a student assembly was taking place. It was months ago, but for me, it will always be yesterday."

Jose looked at Jackson, curious about where this was going, "Of course, who hasn't?"

"Well," Jackson continued, "that's where I worked as the high school coach. I was in the auditorium when the mayhem happened."

Tears were rolling down his cheeks.

"My son and daughter were in the auditorium as well. When the boy started shooting, I sprung out of my seat and yelled for others near me to lie on the ground and hide under the seats. I was in the front row of seating. The shooter was shooting randomly as he moved down to the front of the auditorium. I had remained standing, looking for my two children. I saw Mandy lying on her belly, a few rows from me. I got down on my knees and went to her. I then crawled with her to a side exit from the auditorium to the outside where many other students were slipping out.

After I got Mandy out, I returned to search for my son, Jacob. I stood.

The shooter was looking away from where I was. I saw Jacob lying on his stomach near the front, hiding next to the still body of his classmate. I froze because I didn't want the shooter's attention directed to Jacob's location. But Jacob saw me and called out, "Help me dad." The shooter turned toward the voice and fired at Jacob who had stood to run to me. The shooter gunned Jacob down. A second later, police officers entered and killed the shooter.

"I tell myself repeatedly that if Jacob had not seen me, he would have stayed down. He would be alive today.

"There were also four of my football players who died."

"My heart hurts for you," said Jose, taken aback by the rawness of the story.

Mark continued, "America is not changing. It has been a hard place for non-white folks to live. The school's population was primarily black. The white shooter's motive was to kill blacks. No other reason but to shoot another person because of the colour of his skin. He left many hate messages on social media. No one raised any warnings.

"I couldn't return to the school. They gave me paid leave, and Mandy and I went to grief counselling. People from all parts of Denver, white, black, and brown and rich and poor, tried to help us out along with the so many others who lost someone that day. But I decided I could not stay in the Denver area.

"I had the idea that if I stuck around, I could fight for change. But these mass shootings didn't just start. And after each one, everyone cries out for change in the gun laws, and the gun industry flexes its political muscle to silence those efforts for change.

"And it's not just the gun laws. Many poorer black people cannot vote anymore. There is an evil crossing this country, and poorer black people are in its path. Food is becoming too expensive for ordinary folks and you know how drought and the lack of fresh water is affecting most people who don't have the means to pay for it."

"I know what you're saying," said Jose.

"Well, I quit my job. I couldn't go back to that place. Buried my son, kept my daughter out of school, sold everything, and here we are," said Jackson.

The two men had been standing close to the north wall of Walmart. The wall protected them from a strong southwest wind that was gusting at 55 to 70 mph. Without the wall's protection, they'd be chilled to the bone.

"Jose asked, "What will you do when you get to Mile City?"

"Employers from Saskatchewan come down to hire workers there. Once they hire me, they'll inform their government that they have work for me. The Saskatchewan government will then nominate me to their federal immigration program. Then I'll wait for my permanent resident papers. I'll take anything at first, even working in a restaurant. Once I'm in, I can watch for a better position. I have a college degree."

Jose said, "That's how I'm getting in, the Saskatchewan Nominee Program.

"I've some money to fall back on. Sold things like you did. They say colour doesn't matter so much up there," said Mark.

Jose looked at the man, wondering if he had heard about the family that was killed. *Better he knows*, thought Jose.

"Mark, there's hate there too. Just the other day, a Hispanic family was slaughtered just after they snuck into Saskatchewan. Word is that they were killed because of their brown skin."

Jackson rubbed his chin as this information registered with him. "Fuck, fuck, fuck! What's wrong with people anyhow?"

"People are just scared they'll lose something they figure God gave them, their feeling of superiority," said Jose.

The next morning, Jackson drove off first in his electric vehicle. Kirk followed him out of the parking lot and onto the I25 in his old, gas-guzzling Durango.

Kirk saw Jackson sitting in the driver's seat, no hands on the steering wheel. It was an autonomous car, no driver required.

They had agreed to reconnect in Mile City.

Freda asked Jose, "Nice fella?"

"Seems like it," he said, then he told Freda about the man's personal tragedy.

"Lordy, some people have so much pain in their life. We've been blessed in so many ways." Freda looked back at her children as she reflected on her greatest blessing.

"Jose, turn the air conditioning a little higher. It's still morning, still April, and the heat is already unbearable," suggested Freda.

Jose did as she asked, holding the steering wheel firm because of the heavy wind gusts and the possibility of a buckled area on the highway.

Freda was telling Jose about something she had read last night on her tablet.

"Large ice loss at the North Pole has hurt polar bears," said Freda. "They eat seals, and seal numbers are declining because of the shrinking ice masses. The Inuit eat both seal and polar bear meat and sell off the skins for money."

"So what, Freda? The bears are killers. And who are the Inuit?" asked Jose.

"Come on, Jose, you don't know about the northern indigenous people of Canada?" asked Freda.

"Okay, Freda, you've taught me something new. That's why I love you. You're making me a worldly, knowledgeable man, filled with useless information that I'll never make a buck from."

Freda smiled, "You might just become more curious about your surroundings if you'd take that half-white, half-brown head of yours out of the ground."

"Anyway, polar bears have moved south as the ice mass thaws, while grizzly bears are moving north because of deforestation and drought during the last twenty years. That's a threat to polar bears because, although polar bears are larger and tend to be more aggressive, grizzly bears are known to kill polar bears. Polar bears tend to walk away from a fight, possibly to retain the scant calories available to them.

"The stuff I was reading contemplated whether a polar bear and a grizzly bear might mate and create a new bear species. Polar bears are solitary creatures, but as one species goes north, and the other goes south, interaction between the two may occur. It might not just be a deadly fight for survival and food. You never know, one horny grizzly could mate with a female polar bear."

"Oh, Freda, why do I need to know that?" countered Jose.

12

ONGOING MURDER INVESTIGATION
CORONACH, SASKATCHEWAN

Peter Hamilton exited the detachment building. The two Regina detectives had interviewed him for hours. "Screw them," he said to himself. "The Mounties could not make him give up his boys."

One of his workers picked him up, and he went back to his office.

Sergeant Dagenais told Corporal Jennings they were returning to Regina for now.

"We'll let you know when we'll be down this way again. Meanwhile, listen around and see what the folks around here know. There are posters with the picture of the wrist band you can put up around the area. That scoundrel Hamilton knows who did it."

Lyle agreed. He wanted to sink his teeth into this case. He expected the detectives needed the detachment's help. Members of the Major Crimes Unit were always up to their eyeballs in unsolved cases. This case would be a top priority, but the others also needed their attention. Lyle knew if he helped solve this one, a man like Dagenais would be very appreciative.

Lyle told Dagenais, "I'll let you know what we find out here. I'm going to go back to the area where the bodies were found and scout about on horseback."

∼

LYLE CHECKED the horse's girth strap twice to ensure it was tight and secure. He brought the reins over the quarter horse's head and onto its neck. Grabbing a handful of mane along with the reins in his left hand, he slipped his left foot into the stirrup then swung his right foot up and over the saddle to slip his right foot into the other stirrup. He took the reins in both hands.

Lyle learned to ride in Nova Scotia at his grandfather's farm.

This horse, Whitey, was borrowed from a local rancher. Whitey was calm, good-natured and easy to handle. Lyle had parked the borrowed truck and horse trailer on a trail off the highway before setting off to the crime scene on Whitey's back.

While riding, he tried imagining what had happened. The little girl got separated from her family in the dark. They stopped when they realized she was missing. The family wouldn't have split up in the dark. They wouldn't have wanted to lose another member. The father set off and retraced their steps in search of the little girl. Strangers appeared on ATVs. The father could not locate the little girl and returned. He found men threatening his family. He was gunned down with the others.

Why were there people out on their ATVs in this area in the dark? They discourage night driving in the badlands. This is dangerous terrain in the dark. Poor visibility increases the possibility of a rollover or a crash into large rocks.

Maybe these people, most likely men, were drunk and out for a little risky fun? Or, they were out for a specific reason, like trafficking weapons or drugs? This area is so close to the border. A lot of border smuggling happens in the Big Muddy Valley because it's so desolate.

So sad; they were fleeing the US for a better life in Canada. *Fuckers*, he thought, *I'm going to get the evil bastards.*

When he reached the area where the bodies were found, he looked about. There was a lot of ground to cover. It was 9 AM. There was about ten hours of sunlight left. Whitey, with periodic rests, was good for about 8 hours of riding. The terrain was rocky, so Lyle had no plan to push him hard.

Lyle planned to ride up to the rises. From the higher points, he would have a better look at the area below.

What was he looking for? Those fucks had to be out here for a reason. Maybe they had a hiding place? Where do people hide things in the Big Muddy? The outlaws from yesteryear used the sandstone caves found on the side of the buttes and steep cliffs. The cave entrances are shaped like an upside-down V.

For hours, Lyle rode up to high points in the area. Then he used his binoculars to look around. Sighting cave entrances, he'd ride down to check them out. One cave entrance showed recent activity. There were ATV tracks and footprints on the dusty ground. Candy wrappers and empty beer cans were strewn about.

Lyle dismounted. The sun was in the middle of the sky. This time of year, mid April, it was about 3 PM. The sun shone in Lyle's eyes. It was warm out. However, he felt chilled when he entered the dark cave. He pointed his flashlight around, and searched the interior.

There was a small mound of rock just to the right of the entrance. He bent down and pushed the rocks aside. Underneath it all, he found a wooden box. Inside he found the automatic rifles, hand guns, and ammunition.

∽

THE NEXT DAY, Lyle returned with the Regina detectives and a forensic team.

"This is a big deal," said Sergeant Dagenais. "The killers were out here smuggling. They either smuggled the weapons over the border themselves or took a handoff from smugglers. Great work, Lyle."

Lyle was pleased with himself, but he was not finished.

"Sergeant, I'm going to be asking folks from around here if they have noticed any suspicious activity. People in these parts know what goes on in their backyard."

"Do that, Lyle. I appreciate what you're doing," said Dagenais.

Lyle was pleased to have the opportunity to do detective work. If he were the one to discover who the murderers were, there was no telling what his next posting might be. Maybe, in plainclothes, in a place like Calgary or Vancouver, who knows?

When he got home, Anita told him he was to phone his superior right away.

Lyle phoned his Staff Sergeant. "What's up Sergeant?" he asked.

With Anita listening nearby, he said, "Yeah, well, I'm disappointed. No, well, I'm not sure I want that. Can I get back to you?"

He got off the phone. He was angry.

"They're screwing me over. I earned a promotion. What bullshit?"

Anita was eager to know what took place. "Please, Lyle, please tell me what that was about."

"My promotion is not coming right now. And they want to post me to Wakaw, Saskatchewan, another remote three-person detachment."

At that moment, Anita thought only of herself. "Wow, Wakaw's only an hour from Saskatoon," she rejoiced.

"Anita, you selfish princess. You don't even care that I'm not being promoted."

"Oh Lyle, I'm sorry. I was just looking at the positives of an unpleasant situation."

"Bullshit, you were just thinking about yourself. It's always about you."

Lyle went to the bedroom and changed out of his uniform. He put on a coat and left the house without speaking.

He walked for several miles in the dark, thinking about his options. The RCMP had a union now. He would speak to a rep about grieving the Wakaw assignment. A grievance would take six months before a final decision was rendered. That would prevent him from having to leave Coronach right now.

If he wasn't being promoted, he reasoned, staying at Coronach was his best career move. He could help solve the murders. That would be a game changer. Remaining here with such a high-profile investigation was best for his career.

Anita knew before they got married that his career was important to him. She had agreed to join him on his journey in the RCMP. Did that make him the selfish one? So what if it did? He'd grown up wanting to be a high-ranking member. If she had not agreed to support his aspirations, he wouldn't have married her.

When he returned home that night, he told her he was staying put for now. She threw her wine glass at him, went to the bedroom, and locked the door. Early the next morning, she left to go to her folks' place in Saskatoon.

13

SAMMY NELSON
REGINA, SASKATCHEWAN

She entered the grand old hotel through its Victoria Avenue front entrance. The Canadian Pacific Railway built the Hotel Saskatchewan across from Regina's Victoria Park in 1927. Until 1969, it was the tallest building in Regina. At one time, it was as palatial as any hotel in Canada. Over the years, renovations have restored it to being the place to stay in Regina.

Sammy Nelson is at the hotel today as a guest speaker of the Canadian Public Policy Symposium. Seen as the principal architect of Saskatchewan's amazing success in building a green economy, organizers have asked her to inform public policy makers from across Canada about the best practises in developing a green economy.

People have described her as imaginative and a thinker since she was a toddler. Never bored, always reading and curious, she pursued learning with a passion.

Her father had done small motor repairs in and around Outlook. Her mother wrote children's books. She sold them at outdoor markets in neighbouring towns. Sammy was their only child. Her parents pushed her to be independent and a freethinker. They thought following the mainstream restricted one's view of the possibilities. Sammy never worried in grade school, high school, or university about being accepted. Maybe that's why she was always comfortable with her sexuality. When people called her a dike, she smirked and laughed at the offenders.

Many Outlook residents thought her parents were oddballs. People gawked at them when they walked with their three-year-old Sammy all around town. Her parents did not pick her up or push her in a stroller. They expected her to keep pace. The walks continued into her teens. Town folks made negative remarks loud enough so Sammy's parents could hear them. Sammy also heard them as she grew up. Later, her mother explained to her why they took those walks.

"My sweet Sammy, your father, God bless his soul, and I felt those walks were a way to explore Outlook and make you curious about your surroundings. We felt the walks would help you grow up with an enhanced feeling of independence and adventure."

Sammy loved those walks. The walks aided in her development as an outstanding student and in her self-awareness as a gay person. Comfortable in her own skin, she combatted anti-gay sentiment with steadfast confidence. Always calm, mostly happy, she remains devoted to her mother and thinks of her now deceased father as a most wonderful man, as good a parent as there could've been.

She saw Rebecca at a school rally. The rally was to support First Nations' inherent rights. Rebecca was one of the speakers. Sammy thought, *She's a little person with a big voice. Cute as a whistle.*

Sammy always led with her head. Matters of the heart could come later. Sammy saw a voice for her plans in Rebecca. She saw Rebecca as a means to an end.

They met. They talked and shared their ideas. Later they explored each other's sexual appetites and fantasies. Rebecca listened to Sammy's vision of a green Saskatchewan. Sammy listened to Rebecca's desire to have a more just society. They blended their thinking into a smart way to achieve a better future for Saskatchewan. Rebecca would be the visible voice, Sammy, the brains in the background.

Today, at the symposium, Sammy presented her ideas on a progressive green economy. Afterwards, she took a few questions from the small crowd in attendance.

"Hi, Sammy, my name is Belinda and I'm from Winnipeg. Please tell me what you feel are the key investments in your remarkable Saskatchewan success."

Sammy answered, "The first is leadership. You need a passionate voice telling the truth and expressing urgency. That person must be courageous. We have Premier Mahon, who has exemplified that type of leadership. And Saskatchewan people have invested in her. Recently, seventy-three percent of people surveyed indicated that they trusted the direction she was taking Saskatchewan.

"You also need to spend public money in the right way. In Saskatchewan, our predecessor left us with a moderate deficit and an enormous debt. I'm not going to badmouth them on their fiscal management. I'll only say this—our priorities on spending are different; we are running larger deficits and our debt has grown. Our Moody's credit rating has fallen because, at the beginning, we borrowed lots of money. But Rebecca and her cabinet never wavered in their belief that money spent well would cause a significant growth in the economy and increase government revenue in order to pay off the accrued debt. Our credit rating has improved. Government revenue has been increasing, and our economy is booming.

"Saskatchewan has raw resources that the rest of the world needs. Since the beginning of the Russian conflict in eastern Europe, worldwide grain shortages have been prevalent. Saskatchewan has been called a bread basket.

"Our farmers' crops have been very reliable because our earlier federal and provincial governments had the foresight to dam rivers like the Saskatchewan and Souris rivers. We have two large, healthy bodies of water in Lake Diefenbaker and Rafferty and smaller lakes in the Qu'Appelle Valley and Buffalo Pond north of Moose Jaw. Our predecessor, working with our federal government, expanded irrigation throughout central Saskatchewan allowing farmers to use the hot weather and sturdier crops to produce record crops and be able to export our grains with excellent profits.

"Now, there are federal government restrictions on how much fertilizer farmers can use. Farmers feel they could get even greater yields if these restrictions were lifted. This is a quandary for our provincial government.

"Our federal government imposed a 30 percent reduction of fertilizer use by Canadian farmers effective from 2030 on. That's because nitrous oxide gas is produced when the fertilizer soaks into water or soil. The use of fertilizer increased by 71 percent between 2005 and 2019 resulting in fertilizer-related emissions of nitrous oxide rising by 54 percent in Canada. From a global warming perspective, nitrous oxide is a gas 365 times more potent than carbon dioxide.

"The NGP recognizes how vital potash is for our economy. Saskatchewan potash mines produce the most potash in the world, about 28 percent of the total. Potash is used to make fertilizer. Saskatchewan grain farmers use fertilizer to help feed the nearly billion people on our planet who are starving.

"And for many impoverished nations whose farmland soil is drying from global warming, fertilizer applied after a harvest of cereal crops is needed to restore phosphorous and potassium in the soil.

"We are spending money in partnership with the federal government and the private sector to research ways to reduce fertilizer gas emissions by adding new compounds to the mix that will mitigate the nitrous oxide interaction with water and the soil.

"Saskatchewan has been at the forefront of investing public money in mining rare earth minerals. These minerals are crucial for building wind turbines, electric vehicles, cell phones, and many other green economy products. The trade-off, of course, is the footprint left by any mining, but it's not even close to the damage to our environment by using fossil fuels.

"Our provincial government has placed its trust in Prime Minister Pauline Gervais. The federal government recently unveiled a green building strategy that includes engaging provincial and private sector investments. It has unleashed a boom in green building and construction jobs. It includes rebates for new green housing.

"Finally, next to closing fossil fuel mining, taking gas-guzzling cars off our streets and highways, and providing car buybacks on older fuel-burning cars, we have invested in green economy manufacturing industries like the battery-making plant at Coronach."

Suddenly, a group of five men rose from their chairs in the back and started hollering.

"You fucking women are traitors to Saskatchewan and Canada. And you, Sammy Nelson, are a dike. We're out of work because of you bitches. Closed the oil rigs on us, leaving us to claim Employment Insurance benefits. Then you offer us retraining. For God's sake, we're in our fifties. Training for another job ain't worth it."

Two of the more aggressive men headed to the side stairs up to the stage. As they stepped on the stage, the panel members fled for safety. Except Sammy. Sammy was tall, athletic, and intimidating. Wielding a chair at the two men, she yelled, "Get the fuck off this stage or else one of you is gonna be carried off and the other's balls will be as swollen as watermelons."

The two men looked at each other, then they backed off. Hotel security arrived, and the five men fled the hotel.

"Okay, everyone, I'll take more questions," said a calm Sammy.

They served drinks and dainties afterwards. Sammy mixed with the group, but she had her eyes on the woman who'd asked the first question. She went to her, and they talked for a while. The other woman left the room. Shortly after, Rebecca did the same.

Someone in the room had observed the interaction and followed Rebecca when she left. He wore smart glasses, which held a camera. He followed Rebecca up the elevator, taking pictures when he could. Sammy was unaware of him. The last picture was of the two women meeting at a hotel room and then going in together.

14

TEMPORARY STAY
MILES CITY, MONTANA

Jose Kirk drove his vehicle to where Interstate highways 25 and 90 intersected. Continuing north, he exited 25 and got on Interstate 59 North.

Smoke filled the air. It was coming from a massive fire in Yellowstone Park. The park was a considerable distance to the west of them.

"Freda, it's as if the earth is ablaze."

Combustion was sucking the oxygen from the air, feeding the fires, and spreading them in a widening path.

Jose continued, "Soon, we'll only have black, toothpick-like trees in the forests. Smell the charred wood in the smoke. It can't be good for our lungs."

Freda replied, "Just keep going north. There's not a lot of forests in Montana. We'll be putting these fires behind us soon enough."

The smoke slowly dissipated as they entered the eastern Montana plains. The terrain was grassy and hilly. There were cattle herds grazing in the fields. They saw a sign pointing east saying, "Little Bighorn."

Jose chuckled, "That's where Custer and his men got their asses kicked. It's rare in the United States that it happened to the white man."

Freda scolded him, "Jose, have some respect. You, of all people, saying such a thing. Back in La Cruces, you spent your life trying to be just like a rich white guy."

"Okay, Freda. I was just kidding."

They approached Miles City from the south. Just to the west, they could see the Yellowstone River flowing through a valley.

Entering the wide Main Street that ran north and south, they could see it was not a big place.

"Look," Manuel pointed from the back seat at a mushroom-shaped structure with a long stem and the words Miles City written across it. A steel water tower stood at the north end of the city.

Jose drove down Main Street watching for Lynch Street, named after a famous racing car driver from Miles City.

When he found the street, he turned left and stopped in front of their rental place. Everyone stared at it. They were all underwhelmed.

Victoria spoke first, "Dad, it's tiny. Look at all the weeds. No one has cut the lawn this year."

The owner had not maintained the little house clad in composite siding. It looked like a robin's nest with grass and weeds growing high against the siding.

Jose felt the tension in the car. "Hey, guys, rental properties that didn't require a long-term lease were hard to find. I'm paying $2,500 a month for this."

Freda looked at Jose then looked again at the house. She turned to the kids and said, "Let's get out of the car and see what the inside looks like."

Manuel let Charlie out and he immediately took off to do his business. The kids followed him.

Jose used the key at to the side door to open up the house and let Freda go in first. "Yikes," she shouted. Like the outside, the inside was a mess. There was dust on furniture, cobwebs in the corners, and smudges on the windows. The floor of the only bathroom was sticky, the tub dirty, and the toilet unflushed with a smelly, urine-coloured bowl and a broken seat. The house had a musty smell in it.

"Jose, we're paying $2,500 monthly for this dump?" she groaned.

"Yes, my dear, $2,500 a month."

∽

MARK JACKSON DROVE his electric car into the Best Western Hotel parking lot. A few years ago, the motel had closed. The parking lot was filled with other vehicles bearing licence plates from Texas, Oklahoma, New Mexico, and Colorado.

It was dark. There were no lights in the parking lot.

"Mandy, stay close to me until we get the lay of the land," said Jackson. He got out of the car.

"You can bet on that, Dad," she replied as she scanned the decrepit building and overgrown surroundings. She got out of the car and stretched her long legs. She was wearing a sweater and tight blue jeans that showed off her stunning figure.

She looked at her handsome father. "Are we really thinking of staying here?"

Jackson responded, "Honey, the hotels are all booked, and there are no long-term rental properties that I can afford. Friends back home told me about this place, that it was run by honest folks, and that it was safe. It'll have to do until we get the papers to enter Canada. Just stay close."

A black man in his 60s or there about appeared. "Hello, there," he called out as he approached them. "I'm Chester Mack from Texas. And you are?"

Jackson introduced himself and Mandy and said that they were looking for shelter for a while.

Mack grunted, "Most people who drive into the lot are looking for shelter. It was only two years ago that a group of us old black guys from a town near El Paso came up here to escape the Texas heat. We told each other we'd try our luck in Canada. No one told us about all the red tape we had to cut through to get into Canada. Too old, we were told, and no family ties. Canada denied our entry. Instead of heading back to Texas, we squatted on this here property. Found out that no one was paying property taxes, so we paid what was owed. Here in Montana, you can make a legitimate claim on a property if you pay the taxes, maintain it, and occupy it.

"So, we spent what money we had on fixing up this place. There ain't a lot of rules in Montana for running a public accommodation facility. We just needed to meet building standards, have potable water, have a waste water disposal system, and keep hygienic conditions. So, we run this place more like a bare-bones boarding house than a motel. We do this to help folks like yourself. Just old guys wanting to help. We're too old—we're not looking to get rich; we just need to get by. It's not the Ritz, but we fixed it as best we could. All we ask is that you pay $50 a night into the pot."

"That's reasonable," said Mark.

"How old is your girl?" asked his host.

"Seventeen."

"That's good cause, if she was a minor, the child protection folks would grab her from you. Folks with minors hide their children when they come snooping about here.

"So, are you willing to pay $50 for a room? You will get hot water, electricity, and heat. There's no internet."

"We don't have a lot of options. Here's $350 for a week."

Mack took the money and told Jackson his room was #110. He provided him with a key attached to a silver bottle opener. Jackson and Mandy moved into their new home.

∼

The Canadian Immigration Office was on Main Street, Miles City. The front office area was comprised of ten cubicles, each having a large screen tablet fastened to a desk. There were two support staff to assist applicants and control lineups for access to the cubicles.

Immigrants applying for entry to Canada could use the large screens to speak virtually with an immigration agent face-to-face. The agents are based in different localities across Canada. Applicants require their own device to send and receive documents.

Jose Kirk entered the packed office and lined up for a cubicle. He had all the required documents except his permanent residency card, which would be issued by the Canadian federal government.

After being in a line for three hours, an office worker showed him to cubicle 5. He placed his Saskatchewan Nominee approval forms and his employment offer from the University of Regina on a desk.

A woman appeared on the screen.

"Hello, my name is Heidi and my personal ID number is 85143. Please give me the application number provided to you when your application was confirmed as received."

Jose provided her with the number.

"Mr. Jose Kirk, is that correct?" she asked. "What is it you're inquiring about today?"

Jose answered, "The status of my application. We are waiting in Miles City for approval so we can cross the border."

The immigration officer asked in a sterile, nasal voice, "Why are you in Miles City? You initiated your application in La Cruces, New Mexico."

Suddenly there was a commotion in the cubicle next to his. A woman was shouting loudly, "It has been six months since I arrived here. Saskatchewan nominated me under the Express Entry program a year ago. I needed to have enough money to support myself while I settled and found a job. Your delays are eating away at my necessary funds. They told me my job experience was in demand in Saskatchewan. And you tell me my permanent residency isn't signed off on yet."

There was a pause in her shouting. The immigration officer must have been replying. Then Jose heard another outburst of anger. "You tell me I should have remained in New Mexico until I had the document. For God's sake, my house burned to the ground, water shortages were getting worse, my employer went out of business, and the heat had become unbearable; and you think I should've stayed? Look, you guys get off your asses and sign off. I have children here, and we're living in squalor."

Jose and his immigration officer remained silent during the woman's outburst. Shortly, Jose saw a large white woman exit the cubicle. Jose looked into the screen in front of him and said, "We sold our house. It was a buyers' market there, so we took it. We came here because the last person in your department that I spoke to told us everything was in order and the approval would be released shortly."

Jose wasn't sure if the woman on the screen smirked or grimaced. Either way, her response was not helpful. "You got some bad information. We have a backlog of three million applicants. Yours is in the queue. I can't tell you any more than that. Just try to be patient."

∽

JACKSON and his daughter slept okay their first night. The room was clean, although the beds sagged. They had their own bedding and towels.

The next day, Jackson went to the local Lutheran Church to register for the next time Saskatchewan employers come to Miles City to recruit workers. There was a woman from Regina giving an information session on life in Saskatchewan. Her name was Judy, and she was from a non-profit organization called Regina Welcomes You. Mark stayed for the session.

She told the dozen attendees that Saskatchewan had more jobs than workers. The province had weaned off fossil fuel dependency. They shut down the oil rigs and coal mining. They lost many jobs because of this, but newer, cleaner, better-paying jobs started springing up all over the province. This created a big shortage of workers, which is why employers come to places like Miles City in the United States to recruit skilled labour.

She then described the process to enter Canada. First, she emphasized that not everyone was eligible for the Saskatchewan Nominee Program. People with a criminal record were disqualified. Applicants needed an updated United States passport proving they were American citizens.

She explained, "They speed up the process up for those who meet a minimum threshold of funds they are bringing into Canada. The more self-reliant you are, the more skilled you are, the faster the process is for nomination. These situations are known as being eligible for Entry Express.

"Even if you have received a Saskatchewan Nomination, you cannot enter Canada until you have a permanent residency approval. Of course, you can enter Canada under temporary resident status, but you cannot work.

"The process time, the wait time, for a nominee approval issued by Saskatchewan is 71 to 100 days. Most of you already have your nomination.

"The main backlog is the federal government's approval time for the permanent residency document. I know many of you are in Miles City because you could no longer tolerate the climate conditions and gun violence in your states, and I can understand that. But you need to have resources to remain here or move where you can get a job. The eastern Montana job market is not very good. There are lots of jobs east of here around Williston, North Dakota, where oil fracking is taking place. Consider going there and waiting for your papers. You should be able to find work.

"Once you enter Canada as a permanent resident, you must fulfill your residency obligations. That means being present in Canada for at least 730 days within a five-year period.

"Saskatchewan is an expensive place to live. Wages are great but the economic boom from the green economy has made homes pricey as people move into the province from all over the world. There are more buyers than sellers. Builders can't build fast enough. Houses sell within days of listing. It's difficult finding homes to rent. It's easier in rural Saskatchewan than in the cities. The employers who come down here will have their businesses in both rural and cities. Ask your potential new employer what the housing situation is in the area where he's offering work.

"Many of you know about Canada's Public Health system. For many of you, it's one reason why you want to immigrate to Canada. Apply for a Saskatchewan Health Card immediately. It can take up to three months to receive it. If, after you arrive at your destination and you or someone in your family gets sick and you don't have your card yet, please contact an immigration non-profit like Regina Welcomes You, and they will help you. There are non-profits like the one I work for in areas across the province.

"You will also have to get a Saskatchewan driver's license within 90 days of your arrival. You may not enter Saskatchewan with a gas or diesel vehicle. Only visitors can because they are not staying. In Saskatchewan, car dealers can sell only electric vehicles. When a Saskatchewan resident wants to purchase a new or used vehicle, it can only be an electric one. The Saskatchewan government buys gas or diesel vehicles from owners on a buy-back program. They pay the seller fair value. This buyback does not apply to new residents to the province. If you bring your fuel-operated vehicle in and try to register it and purchase insurance, you won't be able to do so. Without registration and insurance, you cannot operate your vehicle. You're better off selling it here."

There was low grumbling from within the group.

Judy continued, "It is what it is. There are car dealers in the Miles City area who will buy your vehicles. Of course, you will not receive what they're worth. The dealers buy them, then transport them south to sell at a good profit.

"Many people hire transport to the border where their new employer meets them and takes them to where they're headed in Saskatchewan.

"That's all I have for you. I'll just be over at the table if any of you want to talk to me."

Jackson knew that Saskatchewan did not need a football coach, but he felt sure he could convince an employer in the hospitality industry to nominate him. He signed up for the next employer forum.

15

PODCASTING
REGINA, SASKATCHEWAN

"Before you interview me, Allan, tell me about your podcast experience," said Wong.

"Sure, Peter, I'd like that."

Walker told him he started it years ago, after the United States had elected their first demagogue, personality-over-policy, autocratic-leaning president.

"I left the United States and moved first to Toronto and then to Regina. I wanted a smaller community to live in." Laughing, he said, "It seems thousands of others had the same idea because Regina's population has grown from 200,000 people to 275,000 since I arrived."

Walker told Wong that, when he started, 38 percent of Americans and Canadians listened to podcasts about eight times a week. Most did it while listening at home. But with cars being built with smarter accessories like voice-responding computers, more and more people turned to delayed podcasts as their primary source of news. Podcasts appeared on Facebook, mainstream news broadcasting internet platforms like CNN, and many other social media sites. The beauty of podcasts for many is that they can listen to them to whenever they like. The listener has control. It's not breaking news, it's more like just-in-time news. Today, 55 percent of Americans and Canadians listen to podcasts about 20 times in a week.

"Of course, anyone with a message has access to podcasting, and more and more fake news and conspiracy stories dominate the market. My podcast, now the most listened to in North America, has countered those movements. I refer to it as fighting the lies."

Wong asked, "Why is your podcast so popular? There are so many options. Why do people choose to listen to you?"

"Because my podcast is bringing listeners updates on the most current and accurate threats to mankind like climate change and right wing extremism."

"Allan, what did you do in the United States?" asked Wong, hoping to confirm Walker's real identity.

Walker lied, "Small news reporting in a rural area. Peter, we have to start the interview."

So Wong spoke about deforestation.

"Trees are carbon sinks. A carbon sink is anything that absorbs more carbon from the atmosphere than it releases. Trees take carbon dioxide out of the air, hold on to the carbon and release the oxygen into the air. Fewer trees means less carbon is being taken out of the air. In addition, cutting down trees ruins the soil, making it drier and more exposed to the air. Carbon in the soil is then exposed to the atmosphere. When that happens, carbon dioxide is produced and released into the atmosphere. More carbon dioxide in the air means more global warming.

"Rainforests take in carbon dioxide all year around. So, cutting trees in the Amazon rainforests to make room for agriculture removes year-round carbon sinks. Agricultural activities that replace the natural carbon sinking process with raising cattle, for instance, causes more greenhouse emission. Cows expel methane, a greenhouse gas. It's a double whammy to our environment.

"The boreal forest is the planet's oldest forest. It stores a massive amount of accumulated carbon from thousands of years. The Canadian boreal forest is the ecosystem for plants and animals and home to five million Canadians.

"Boreal forests, like that which we have in our Canadian north, need protection. Saskatchewan, where I'm coming to you from, is two-thirds boreal forest and one-third prairie.

That will change to more prairie and less forest if action is not taken.

"The transpiration process where trees absorb water through their roots and then give off water vapour through the pores in their leaves is being changed by the warmer weather. With less water absorbed and more water evaporating, stress is being placed on the trees.

"The warming is making forest renewal more difficult. Natural disturbances like forest fires and insects are no longer part of that renewal but are threats to the forest's continuing existence.

"Trees faced with a lack of water close the pores on their leaves to stop the water escaping and evaporating. By doing this, they are not gaining the nutrients needed to grow. Growth is stunted, trees take in less carbon dioxide, and more warming causes more drought.

"The cycle is fires followed by drought where seeds and seedlings don't survive, and forests become prairie grassland. This is happening here in Saskatchewan. There is more prairie now than there was ten years ago. Saskatchewan is losing forests faster than they can be regrown. More insects threatening to plant life appear. Wild life is being displaced."

Wong continued until his time is up.

WONG LOOKED at the twelve spring sessional students sitting in the university classroom. There was an even split between Saskatchewan resident students and foreign students. This was a first-year science class on the environment.

"Hello, my name is Doctor Peter Wong. Today, our first class together, I'm going to take you to my past and my beginnings teaching about our environment."

He looked around the room to see if he had caught their attention. It seems he had. He learned a long time ago that students were interested in knowing about their teacher.

"Is that okay with you folks?"

The students nodded their interest.

"Back in 1988, right here in Saskatchewan, the government of the day proposed to dam a small river named the Souris. Its source is just north of Weyburn, Saskatchewan, and wanders south past Minot, North Dakota, then back up north into Manitoba. The source is marshland whose water is drawn from snow melt and spring rain.

"The Saskatchewan government worked with the government of North Dakota to dam it. In those days, the water flow from the Souris River varied from year to year. During the drought years, farmers and towns who depended on the water were deprived of adequate water. In other years, flooding occurred affecting the North Dakota city of Minot. To offset these variations in water flow, the Saskatchewan and North Dakota governments agreed to build the Rafferty dam just west of Estevan, Saskatchewan.

"At the same time as the dam was being built, the Saskatchewan government was building the Shand Power Plant at Estevan.

"The Shand Power Plant is an ignite coal burning plant requiring water to cool the turbines. So they built a pipeline from the reservoir created by the dam running to the power plant.

"The environmental outcry in those days wasn't about spending public money on burning coal for energy, the most lethal producer of greenhouse gas known to humankind. Wetlands and flooding 16,000 acres of good farmland were the focus of the protests.

"The reason I tell you about that event is to provide you with an understanding of just how recent it has been since the general population was warned about global warming. Sure, in the 19th century, scientists studied and discussed among themselves the global warming trend, but warnings of the dire consequences did not become public until the 1990s."

Wong spoke until the class time was up, then he went home and made his face-to-face report to his Washington handler —but not until he had schemed about how he would stall again.

PART II

SUMMER, 2032

16

HAIL STORM
MILES CITY MONTANA

The summers in Miles City are hot, dry and sunny, with long summer days from June 15th to August 15th. After August 15th, daylight decreases and the evening darkness settles in earlier.

The wind blows from the west every day, on average, about 20 MPH. Locals tell the migrants that it is a helluva lot hotter, drier, and windier than ever before. They tell them a heat wave hits Miles City in mid-June and remains until mid-September. The storms have never been fiercer.

What trees the semi-desert area had are dying from insect infestation and lack of moisture. The growing season in 2022 was 151 days, and now, it's 160 days. Area farmers plant more winter wheat, and harvesting is earlier than ten years ago.

The climate is changing in eastern Montana. It is getting warmer every year.

Jose Kirk was attending an evening session on Canadian Immigration settlement being hosted by the Lutheran Church. People were fanning themselves to keep cool. He saw Mark Jackson sitting in a church pew several rows behind him. The two men nodded to each other.

The moderator was Judy again from Regina Welcomes You.

Judy asked people in the audience to share their current circumstances. The first person who raised her hand was a woman from Central American. She spoke only Spanish and told her story with the help of a translator.

She was fleeing violence and poverty in her homeland. She had walked and jumped on trains with only the clothes on her back carrying water and a bit of food for her and her three young children. Missions on the journey provided food. Sometimes, she raided gardens. She had no money. The Lutheran Church in Miles City was helping her out.

She told everyone that Canada will not accept refugees passing through the United States because of the Safe Third Country Agreement between the two countries. Under the Agreement, refugee claimants are required to request refugee protection in the first safe country in which they arrive. There are exemptions. She has been trying to qualify for an exemption under family reunification. Her sister lives in a place called North Battleford, Saskatchewan.

She was pleased to tell everyone that her approval documents have come, and she is heading north this week.

Chester Mack, the Texas man from the motel where Jackson was staying, rose to speak.

"I came up with a group from Texas. Most of 'em are up in Canada now. But they have declined me entry. Ain't got the skills they're looking for, ain't got the money, too old, I guess. So me and a few like me are helping folks out at a run-down, abandoned motel. We're safe there and have purpose. Means a lot, you know, having purpose when you're old."

He sat down and was followed by the woman who had the outburst three months earlier at the Immigration Office. She told them about her wait for her permanent resident documents.

"I think," she said, "they will issue my documents soon.

Several American migrants told why they were heading to Canada. They stated reasons like PAP's disenfranchising initiatives, mass murders, lack of medical insurance, water and food shortages, and declining job opportunities. No one came right out and said it was climate change. But those jobs losses and the food and water shortages were because of intense heat waves, devastating floods and storms, drought, and dried up soil.

Judy thanked those who spoke. She advised that settlement and English language services are available in most of the larger communities in the province. She used Regina Welcomes You as an example and described its programs and services.

She repeated her previous advice regarding electric vehicles. "People moving to Saskatchewan who drive gas and diesel vehicles cannot register them in Saskatchewan."

After the information session was over, Jose approached Jackson to talk. Coffee and doughnut in hands, the two sat down to visit.

"Good to see you, Jose. How are you?" asked Mark.

"Fine, I've got our entry documents. We will head north next week. How about you?"

"I'm okay. I've been to those employer recruitment events. Been offered temporary worker status for a farm job way up in a place called Big River, Saskatchewan. But I didn't accept. They wouldn't let Mandy come with me and when the seasonal work is over, I'd have to return to the States.

"There's this coffee company called Tim Hortons that is hiring. I spoke to an owner of several of their franchises. He told me they usually hire younger workers from the Philippines, but he was interested in me to manage an overnight shift because I'm a big man and I'm mature. Told me he had watched me play in the NFL and had been a fan. It's not great pay, but my plan is to study so I can teach up there so the job might be just right. He told me he'd nominate me under the

Saskatchewan Nominee Program, like the way you're getting in. Told me it would be about a year before I'd get in."

Jose said, "That's a little longer than what it has taken us. What are you going to do while you wait? You can't keep staying in Miles City in that abandoned motel."

"No, Mandy's bored, and she needs something to do. She needs to complete grade 12, but she wants to do that in Saskatchewan. She talks about working, but with so many migrants here, there are no jobs available.

"Ever hear of Williston, North Dakota?" asked Mark. "It's 160 miles east of here."

Jose replied, "Yeah, that's the place whose population has tripled in the last twenty years because of an oil boom.

"Yes, well, there are 2,300 job openings in a city of only 37,000 people. We can go there once the Tim Hortons' owner gets my nomination approved. We'll finish the rest of the immigration process there and go north at the port of entry near Estevan, Saskatchewan."

Jose looked at Mark and asked, "Are you and Mandy interested in coming over for a BBQ tomorrow night. Looks like you could use some home cooking."

Mark smiled and said, "You bet. Don't suppose you'd mind me bringing a bottle of bourbon?"

Jose returned the smile with one of his own, "Absolutely. Come at 6 PM. Here's our address."

～

THE DAY HAD BEEN hot and muggy instead of the normal hot and dry. People saw low clouds to the west of the city.

Some local folks in the coffee shop said, "It hasn't been this muggy for a while. Maybe some rain will fall," they added hopefully.

Mark had learned that, up here in the north, the number one topic discussed at the coffee shop was the weather.

Mandy and Mark left the coffee shop to browse about town. When it was time, they drove to the Kirk's place.

He parked in front of the Kirk's place a little after 6 PM. It was overcast, with threatening dark clouds to the west of them. It cooled the air a bit, but it was still humid.

Freda and Jose, and Charlie the dog, met them at the door. The house was immaculate. Mark complimented Freda on their home.

Freda answered, "You should have seen it when we first came. The landlord should be paying us to live here. The four of us worked hard to make it decent.

"Children, our company is here. We have air conditioning. Jose worked to make it work. He's good at fixing things. The kids have been inside on their tablets because it's been so hot."

Victoria and Manuel arrived and greeted their guests.

"Come around to the back. We've mowed the grass and trimmed the trees back there. I've used my landscaping skills to make it a nice sitting area with shade," said Jose.

And it was nice. The tall cottonwoods and poplar trees had been trimmed. There was a pile of logs and branches that came from the trimming and some dying trees Jose had cut down. The grass was still brown, but there aren't any weeds mixed in with it.

"I cut them down." Jose pointed at the log piles. "Some are dry from being dead for a while but we can't have a fire to burn them because there's such a risk of the fire getting away on us. With the winds, an ember might set the old part of the town on fire," said Jose.

"We've got a gas BBQ so that we can cook these nice Montana steaks. Freda has done some cold salads because it's too hot for cooking," continued Jose.

Mark handed the bottle of bourbon to Jose. "Mandy can drive and I can drink," chuckled Mark.

Jose took the bottle and asked Mark if he'd like to cool down with a beer first.

"Won't say no," replied Mark. "Mandy, go visit with Mrs. Kirk. You're not with women very often these days, and I want to propose something to Mr. Kirk."

"Sure, dad," she said.

When Jose returned with the two beers after starting the BBQ, Mark proposed a win-win deal for the two of them.

"Jose, we should trade vehicles. You will need an electric car in Canada and the dealers will soak you for every dime they can get. I need money now. The three months of rent for that dump and having to buy restaurant food for Mandy and me is eating away at what little money I brought with me. My electric vehicle is only three years old and has 50,000 miles on it. I've maintained it and there's nothing wrong with it. I figure, if we were in Denver, I could get near $20,000 for it. Now your Durango is what, a 2023 model?"

"It's a 2020," Jose corrected him, "with 150,000 miles on it. The engine is in good shape because I service it myself."

"Okay, older than I thought. In La Cruces, the weather is dry and cars don't rust, so the body is in great shape. If you pay me $15,000 for my car and throw in the Durango, you can have the electric car. A local dealer will give you maybe $1,000 on a trade and you'll pay a lot more for an electric car."

Jose pondered the offer. He recognized that Mark was being very generous.

"What about space? I've things in the Durango that I'm bringing north with me that I couldn't fit in the U-Haul."

"Jose, you'll have the same problem, regardless. You'll have to spend a ton of money on a larger vehicle, unless you discard some of what you have. What you discard cannot possibly be worth the extra cost of a larger vehicle. You'll just have to shave away some of what you're taking. You'll be able to buy what needs replacing in Regina," said Mark.

Jose reached out to shake Mark's hand. "You're right; you've got a deal."

The night darkness was settling in as they finished their meal. Because it had been so dry, there were no mosquitos bothering them.

Freda looked up at the sky and pointed at the dark clouds. "Look at the awesome cloud pattern. It's like dog paws are roaming the sky," she commented. Off in the distance, a bolt from blue flash came out of the side of a thunderstorm cloud and lit up the sky.

"A storm is coming our way. Mandy, would you like to help me put the kids to bed and then we can have a cup of tea in the kitchen?"

"Sure, Mrs. Kirk."

The fellas were drinking bourbon and their voices were getting louder. The two men got along really well.

In the kitchen, Freda poured Mandy a cup of speciality herbal tea.

"Mandy, how come you've no mom?"

Mandy didn't reply right away. She collected her thoughts first. Thinking of those days with her mom, when she was only a child, was a mix of fond memories and a painful past.

"During the Covid-19 pandemic, my mother caught the virus. She died in 2020. She had been vaccinated, but she was a diabetic. She spent months in the hospital before dying. I was only five, but I still remember her sweet smell and soft voice."

"Oh, you poor child. You know, honey, we haven't spent a lot of time getting to know each other. You are such a beautiful young woman. And you have so much ahead of you. If I can help you in moving past the loss of your mother and brother, I will."

"That's very kind of you, Mrs. Kirk."

"Freda, please, call me Freda."

"Mrs. Kirk, I mean, Freda. I'm in trouble." Mandy's lip trembled when she said that.

"Is someone at the motel pestering you?" asked Freda.

"No, that's not it. It's just boring every day. We get up, eat stale muffins with coffee, then go into town. Dad does his thing to get into Canada, and then we eat a hot meal, pick up more day-old pastry and bread and go back to the room."

Mandy cried. "It's not the motel, it's me. I've gotten myself in a mess."

"Tell me, child. I promise to listen and then the two of us can see what we can do to fix it," said Freda.

"My dad had warned me not to engage with people I don't know over the internet. One day, when dad went into town, I stayed behind. Through a social media website, I met a guy. He seemed nice at first. His name was Robert. Told me he was 18. We just messaged back and forth.

"We just talked at first about being our age. Then one day, he encouraged me to do a face-to-face call. When I saw him, he was so nice-looking. Said he was from Saskatchewan. I told him that was where we were headed.

"About a month ago, he pressured me to remove my top and bra. He then took a screenshot of me without my permission. The next time during a face-to-face call, he asked me to remove all my clothes. I told him no, but he insisted and I resisted. After a while going back and forth over this, he told me that if I didn't comply, he was going to post the pictures of my breasts online. I've avoided his calls lately, but I'm afraid he's going to expose me on the internet."

Freda went over and hugged the young woman. She had heard of this sextortion.

"Honey, give me your tablet."

Mandy took it out of her purse and gave it to Freda.

"First thing we're going to do is create a file and save all his messaging with you. The next thing is we're going to block any more communications from him. Tomorrow, when you come into town, you come here while your dad does his business. I need help and a companion as well. And while you're here, we can talk about what else to do to make the guy stop.

"I see you took a screenshot of him. That's very good," said Freda.

Mandy hugged Freda back and whispered her thanks.

Outside, the two men noticed a strong wind was building. Rain started falling, A horn started blaring that could be heard throughout the entire community. It was a tornado warning. The two men gathered what was left out from the BBQ and went inside. The little house had a small dirt root cellar. The children were awakened and taken down with Freda, Mandy, and Charlie. There was not enough room for the men. They went to the bathroom on the main floor where the structure was most secure.

Flashes of brilliant lightning followed by the sound of booming thunder split the sky. They heard hail drumming on the roof and on the west side of the house. The wind howled. Then as quickly as it had come, the storm left and silence returned.

"I hope the hail did not damage your new electric car," joked Mark.

Everyone converged in the kitchen to excitedly discuss the storm. Once everyone calmed down, the kids returned to their beds, and Mandy and her father thanked their hosts for a wonderful evening and returned to the motel in the new Durango.

Neither vehicle showed any hail damage.

The next day, there were reports of damage, including to a ranch house. The rancher's grey metal bins were tossed and crushed. Nobody was hurt, but the rancher lost nine horses in the storm.

17

TRAPPINGS

SOUTHEAST SASKATCHEWAN

Corporal Lyle Jennings met the informant in an abandoned farm yard outside Killdeer, Saskatchewan. It was near the Saskatchewan-Montana border. They stood inside a homestead house left in ruins.

The summer sun was too fiery to stand out in the open. Weather experts were declaring this was Saskatchewan's hottest summer on record. The short crunchy brown crops bore this out.

The informant said, "The wrist band belonged to Robert Hamilton, Peter's youngest son. When I worked for the old man, Robert wore it all the time. At the time, he was too young to work there, but he'd show up in the shop after school and hang around until closing time."

"Okay, Doyle, what else can you tell me?" asked the corporal.

"Robert is in Regina somewhere. Someone from Rockglen was there recently. He saw Robert in a Walmart on the east end. Also, the guns you found were owned by the Ole Boys. I know because I was one of them until they talked crazy. Until the murder of that poor family in April, they had done no real harm.

"So, do I get the $5000 reward?" he pressed.

Lyle looked into the man's eyes and saw greed. "No, you get it only if your information leads to a conviction. I need you to do more." He arranged for a warrant to record a conversation between his informant and Peter Hamilton.

Corporal Jennings and his informant met again at the abandoned farmhouse. He gave Doyle a pair of smart sunglasses.

"Doyle, these glasses can film and record just like your cell phone. You only need to look like you're scratching your hair and then, push the small button on the glasses' arm to start the video."

"He'll kill me if he finds out."

"You won't be caught. Practice the motion repeatedly before you meet him.

"He'll want to meet you out in the open where no one else is around. When he picks the location, you inform me. I'll be out there, hidden in the field with my rifle. If I sense you're in danger, I'll fire a warning shot and shout out to warn him off.

"You're going to get him to meet you by telling him you were interviewed by me. Tell him I told you I've got evidence to pin the murders on you and on him. You're afraid. You want his opinion on what you should do. Never be direct with him. Don't appear to be trying to push him to talk. And if he provides nothing for the first time, we'll try again. This is how you'll be able to claim the reward."

Doyle looks apprehensive but agrees to do it.

Doyle and Hamilton are in an open field near Willow Bunch. Jennings lies in a low spot in the field, out of sight.

Doyle had scratched his hair and turned on the smart eyeglasses' recorder all in one smooth motion.

∼

Hamilton asked, "So why does he think it's you and me?"

"Because I was an Ole Boy, and someone in the area pointed a finger at me. You know they found the weapons?"

Hamilton, "Yeah, yeah, but they don't know squat. And you don't tell them squat. Understand?"

Doyle, "For sure Mr. Hamilton. Jennings referred to your son, Robert, and mentioned a wrist band."

Hamilton was agitated, "Don't even talk about that .... don't ... don't even."

Doyle whined, "I'm just trying to inform you about what I was told."

Hamilton, calmer, stated, "There is no way they can connect Robert, no way, unless someone like you blabs his big mouth."

Doyle shifted his feet, "Won't come from me. The Corporal told me they have seen Robert in Regina. Is that where he's hiding?"

This took Hamilton by surprise, "No, the three are supposed to be in Ontario."

Doyle, "That's a good place to be if they have reason to be scarce around here."

Hamilton stiffened into a threatening stance, "Look here, Doyle, my boys are impulsive sometimes and don't think things through, but they're my boys and if you say or do anything that brings the law down on them, you'll pay dearly."

∼

BACK AT THE DETACHMENT, Lyle played the recording for Stu and Fred.

"Fred, I want you to watch Hamilton for a shift and then Stu will relieve you. I believe he didn't know that Robert was back in Regina. I suspect he'll know where to find him there. If he makes a move, follow him. He'll probably head to Regina. He'll want to meet his son. If it happens on your shift, contact me at once and I'll let Sergeant Dagenais know."

Constable Fred Zimmer, driving an unmarked car, parked down the street from Hamilton's Willow Bunch home. It was just after 7 PM. He saw Hamilton get into his big Cadillac SUV and back out onto the street.

Zimmer waited a moment before he followed. Hamilton left Willow Bunch and drove onto Hwy 13 east. The drive to Regina was 191 kilometres. Hamilton was driving fast. The electric unmarked police car did not have difficulty keeping pace.

Zimmer used the wide band radio to advise Jennings what was happening. Lyle phoned Sergeant Dagenais to fill him in. Dagenais alerted the Regina City Police.

Hamilton left Hwy 13 and turned north on Hwy 6 toward Regina. Zimmer continued to follow undetected. The sun was setting in the west as they approached Regina's overpass where Hwy 6 crossed over the Trans Canada Highway. Hwy 6 lead straight onto Albert Street at the southern end of Regina. The sun's crepuscular rays appeared orange against the tall Saskatchewan Government Insurance building in downtown Regina.

Sergeant Dagenais instructed Zimmer to back off. Another unmarked police vehicle took over following Hamilton on Albert Street.

Hamilton continued travelling north on Albert Street through the underpass for the railroad tracks. He turned west onto Dewdney Street and into the North Central neighbourhood.

The neighbourhood was Regina's wrong side of the tracks. There was a lot of crime. The area was improving, but it was still the area where most criminals operated from.

Hamilton parked his car on a side street in front of a small, rundown house. There were a couple of guys sitting on the steps, smoking and drinking.

When Hamilton approached, one of them said, "What the fuck are you doing here, old man?"

Hamilton drew a revolver from the back of his belt and waved it. "Move assholes, this old man means business."

The two guys let him pass.

Once Hamilton was inside, Regina Police cars came from both directions of the street with sirens shrieking. Police cars also came down the back alley. After a short time, men in wife-beater tee shirts come out of the house and into the warm night air, their hands held high.

18

WONG'S DECISION

REGINA, SASKATCHEWAN

Wong contacts Larsen on FaceTime.

"I'm done doing podcasts with Walker for now. He's having a kook on for the next while who is spreading false information about global warming. Walker's your guy, so I'm done with this bullshit cloak and dagger stuff."

"You're right, you are and I have paid your debts off," said Larsen. "But I heard from reliable sources at the university that you're gambling again and losing. Good, I might need you again."

Larsen has his hitman in place. He is an Ole Boy from Swift Current, Saskatchewan. Just one word from Larsen, and Walker would be dead. However, Larsen is holding off for now. He wants to see what Wong will do in the next few days.

Wong might be very useful in the future. Larsen enjoys owning people to use for his evil doings. Larsen knows how to wait; he had spent time in the joint.

They signed off with no signs of cordiality.

Wong's last sessions with Walker were about the bigger causes of greenhouse gas emissions. Gas- and diesel-driven vehicles, old agricultural practices, raising livestock, fossil energy-dependent industries, deforestation, and coal, gas, and oil extraction were all pointed out as the most threatening to our environment.

The message he most wanted the listeners to understand was that climate change was everyone's problem, not just the big offenders. If you are ignorant or indifferent, then learn and become an advocate for cleaner air. Use your democratic vote to help elect green-minded officials. Wong touched on Saskatchewan's success under the NGP in creating a green economy.

He told his audience they could choose an electric car over a gas guzzler, eat food made by processes that didn't add to greenhouse gas emission, and spend your money on products that were made using cleaner methods. Producers will track your spending choices and change their production methods accordingly.

During the last interview, Wong thanked Walker for the opportunity to advocate.

Wong had kept his distance from Walker since he spent the evening at the man's place. Wong hated himself for the deception and betrayal game he was playing.

His own weaknesses could cause the death of a man who overcame his own addiction. He had respect for him; the man he disliked was himself.

Wong had gone to Casino Regina every evening. Ironically, the casino was right across the street from where he grew up.

Soon, his losses piled up, and the income he was receiving from the university did not cover his losses. He knew how to find people willing to lend to him. Regina had its loan sharks. So he borrowed. It was always the same.

As his debt grew, so did his guilt and his despair.

The solution came to him during one of his sessional classes. He had been teaching the students about the failed carbon capture project at the Shand Power Plant. Years earlier, the Saskatchewan Party government and a Conservative federal government invested large amounts of capital to fund a carbon capture project.

Once the project was up and running, the cost of capturing a ton of carbon dioxide was very costly. And, in most years, the project was capturing only 57 percent of the carbon being emitted by the power plant. Yet, the Saskatchewan Party kept promoting it. They told people they could sell the captured and contained carbon dioxide for other industrial uses. The only buyers were oil companies that used it to help extract more oil, creating more carbon dioxide that emitted more greenhouse gas into the atmosphere. Money poured into the project, and all the project did was continue Saskatchewan's reliance on fossil fuels. The project, in the environmentalists' view, was a means through which the fossil fuel industry could claim they were meeting the expectations of regulators and the public. They had sold Saskatchewan people a false bill of goods.

The carbon capture project only ceased when the NGP came to power and ordered it to stop. Governments had spent a lot of money on a losing venture.

Wong thought, *I've been wasting money on a losing venture most of my life. It's just like spending money on something like carbon capture. Gambling was just like that; it was a false bill of goods.*

This had to end. First, he needed to put in motion actions that would save Walker's life and end Larsen's evil once and for all.

Wong wrote an email to Larsen.

"Larsen, you're a scar on society. Prison is where you should be for the rest of your life.

"Should you bring harm to Allan Walker or to me, correspondence and recordings of your vile plan for harming Mr.

Walker will be released to Canadian police, over which you have no influence. As well, the same correspondence will be sent to the New York Times and the Washington Post.

"Arrogant men like yourself believe you can gain control over men like me because we have weaknesses. Yes, I have my addiction but I also have limits to what I'll allow to control my soul.

"Since I first met you, I've recorded our conversations on this small little recording device I hid in my ear. Sure, you took my phone away, but man, are you so arrogant that you'd think an Oxford man wouldn't know about more discreet recording devices? Oxford has a secret spy school. It's in the science departments. Many of the professors were friends of mine. They schooled me on how to use these devices if I ever needed to. I've enough to destroy you. And I will if you do not obey my directives.

"And I've kept all our emails to prove it's you talking in the recordings.

"In closing, no more face-to-face discussions, no more emails, no contact at all, and fuck off."

That was not Wong's complete plan. He intended to release the recordings and emails in due time. Larsen was going to have his Waterloo.

～

JUDY WAS LOOKING FORWARD to meeting a family arriving from Miles City in the next few days. She scrolled down on her laptop to the file for the Kirk family.

Jose Kirk was coming in by way of employer nomination. The University of Regina had hired Jose Kirk to do landscaping for half the year and maintenance in the dormitories for the other half. He was arriving with his wife, two children, and a dog named Charlie.

She had emailed the Kirks with a list of to do's. Charlie needed to have all his shots updated. The Kirks had to have completed arrival forms that included their health records and travel documents. She warned them against trying to bring in any hidden contraband. Canadian Border Patrol have seen an uptick in contraband since the number of American immigrants and refugee asylum seekers increased in the last few years. Smugglers preyed on immigrants and forced them to smuggle drugs and other illegal items for them.

Tonight, Judy was meeting Allan at Victoria's Pub for a drink. It was located on the corner of Victoria Avenue and Hamilton Street.

Allan sat alone at a bistro table when she entered. Judy had hoped Peter Wong would be there. She liked the man.

Judy said, "Turned you down again?"

Allan replied, "Yep, seems he doesn't want to be friends with us."

"How was your day?"

Allan answered, "Mixed. I interviewed that fucking idiot from some place in Texas. Before the interview, we had some small talk. He complained about stronger hurricanes and tornados from the Texas coast, and how much rain was falling and how more flooding was occurring. But he wouldn't acknowledge that the cause was a warming ocean. Then the hypocritical prick called global warming a hoax while I was interviewing him. He had the usual false talking points. Feeds into people's fear about what's happening to their preferred view of life. He's motivated by his self-interest, and the people who agree with him do so because he's saying what they want to hear.

"But I enjoyed slicing his crazy talk like a loaf of bread. You know, arguing with a guy like that helps convince people that climate change is real and as threatening to our survival as Russia's ongoing threat of pushing the button on a nuclear bomb."

"Allan, why don't you consider interviewing an immigrant who has left the United States because of the effects of global warming?"

"Judy, my love, that's a great idea," he replied while sipping his Coca Cola.

A man sat alone across the room, sipping on a beer. His eyes were on Judy and Allan. Later, when the couple got up to leave, he stood as well. He followed them to their home.

19

GOODBYE TO MILES CITY
MONTANA-SASKATCHEWAN

The Kirks are packing to leave. Outside their Miles City, Montana, rental home, they stand talking with Mark and Mandy Jackson.

"Here's the key to the place, Mark. I paid rent to August 1st," said Jose.

"It's so nice to get away from the motel. So kind of you, Jose. It seems you've been able to get everything in the U-Haul and electric car," responded Mark.

"Charlie will complain. He's gonna have less room to wag that big tail of his."

He hitched the trailer to the vehicle. The Kirks will be in Canada in three hours, plus whatever the wait time is at the Regway Port of Entry near Plentywood, Montana.

"Judy will meet us once we arrive in Regina. She's the lady who comes here to give the immigration information at the Lutheran Church," said Jose.

Freda asked Mandy to go inside with her on the pretence she wanted to show her something in the kitchen.

Inside, Freda opened her tablet to a Saskatchewan news platform. She scrolled down past the following headlines:

Water Levels, Farmland Parched in Europe Amid Severe Drought

Saskatchewan Grain Prices Reach Record Highs Due to European Drought and Continuing Conflict in Eastern Europe

Saskatchewan Small Businesses and Farms Benefit from Bank Loans for Green Initiatives

Heat Warnings Continue across Canada amid Scorching Temperatures, Humidity

Robert (picture) Hamilton of Willow Bunch Saskatchewan Taken into Custody for Murder of Illegal Immigrants.

"Look down at the fifth headline with the picture. That's the fella who bullied you online, right?

"Yes ... yes, Freda. Oh my God, they must have his phone with my pictures."

"Yes, honey, but the police won't put it out there. They'll find other girls' pictures too. A creep like that has done this sort of thing before. You needn't worry about him again. He's headed to a place where smart devices are forbidden."

Mandy cried and hugged her friend. "I'm going to miss you so much, Freda."

"Honey, we'll meet in Regina soon enough."

∼

THE KIRKS ARRIVED at the Regway Port of Entry at around noon that day. There were two separate lanes for vehicles to pass through the Canadian customs checkpoint. One was for Canadian residents and transport trucks coming in from the United States. The other lane was for non-residents. The traffic in the first lane moved through the checkpoint quickly and steadily. The non-resident lane, where the Kirks were lined up, was backed up for a mile.

It took three hours to reach the spot where they were greeted by a border immigration official.

The agent came to the driver's side and asked why they wanted to enter Canada. Jose said that they were immigrating to Canada. He provided the agent with all their documents and their American passports. Everyone remained seated in the car.

"Please, sir, step out of the car and open the U-Haul and the trunk."

Jose did as he was told. Another agent appeared with a sniff dog. The agent with the dog opened the back of the vehicle and had the dog sniff for contraband. The kids held tight to Charlie, who had a low rumbling growl deep in his throat. The other dog paid no attention to Charlie.

"Okay, sir, you're all set to go," said the agent.

The highway north to Regina was a rough and narrow road. There were many breaks in the asphalt with chunks scattered across the road. Jose drove cautiously. The highway became much better when it integrated with Highway 39. From there, it was clear sailing into Regina.

Between the border and Regina, there were wind turbines and solar panels spread out across golden fields of wheat.

Freda remarked, "I read that Saskatchewan removed most of the oil pump jacks and replaced them with these turbines and solar panels. The crops are so much better here than what we saw in Montana.

"Saskatchewan farmers use more irrigation systems to water their crops. I read that the water once used for the coal power plants is now used for irrigation. Also, money spent at the power plants has been redirected for research into new farming techniques and technologies."

Jose said to Freda, "Now I'm fully up to date on Saskatchewan farming. So looking forward to my next lesson. What is that going to be about?"

Freda responded playfully, "About how ignorance is bliss."

"Dear Freda, I am in bliss. I'm ignorant, and I'm not worrying about the world."

On a deserted stretch of Hwy 6 beside the abandoned town of Corrine, Jose parked the car. Everyone got out to stretch their legs. They were all struck by how hot it was. Charlie sprang out of the car and ran off to pee and sniff around. The air was filled with the earthy smell of ragweed. Grasshoppers swarmed up around them as they explored the area. Freda cleaned the squashed grasshoppers off the windshield of the car.

When Jose returned to the car with Charlie, he got in and sat back in the seat, savoring the cold air from the car's A/C. Freda finished cleaning the windshield and got in.

"Jose, I heard on my earbuds that a slow-moving storm spawned three tornados and dumped more than 6 inches of rain and hail in Cheyenne, Wyoming. That's where we spent the night in the Walmart parking lot. Cars and trucks were seen floating down the Main Street after the heavy flooding. Telephone poles were cut in half from terrible winds. Eight people are dead, including a deputy sheriff who'd tied himself to a utility pole while trying to save people in a submerged car.

"It's climate change.

"So sad. More and more of these deadly storms are striking areas in the southwest. I imagine Saskatchewan gets their fair share of these types of storms. But Judy said at one of her Miles City information sessions that Saskatchewan is known throughout the world as one place combatting climate change. I wonder how places that do better are negatively impacted by areas that are doing poorly. I imagine the countries that are the big polluters affect us here. And, to avoid a world moving to a point of no return, all countries will have to reduce greenhouse gas."

~

Judy was proud to live in Regina. The city was the capital of Saskatchewan and the second largest city in the province with a population of nearly 300,000 people. The city was located on the traditional lands of Treaty 4 territory. In 1870, representatives of Queen Victoria and the chiefs of the Cree and the Saulteaux First Nations signed the treaty. Regina was also the homeland of the Métis. The city has welcomed European settlers since the 1880s.

Located on flat plains, you can see miles in any direction from Regina. The weather has two extremes, hot summers and frigid winters. Often folks say in jest, that there are only two seasons here, cold dry weather for 8 months, and a warm, comfortable summer for 4 months.

Judy has helped so many new arrivals from foreign countries since she started working at Regina Welcomes You. The city has become a new home to a diverse group of immigrants.

The city has been a place where new housing and business development occurred outside the downtown core. By 2032, fewer employees worked downtown. The Covid-19 pandemic resulted in the trend of many employees working from home. After vaccines mitigated much of the seriousness of Covid-19, not all employees returned to their office work stations, preferring to work from home. Many employers allowed them to. Fewer retail businesses, restaurants, and hotels remained in the downtown core. It wasn't viable to stay.

The city council responded well to the challenges of revitalizing the downtown. They converted smaller office buildings into affordable housing. With unprecedented population growth and demand outpacing the supply of suburban homes, they encouraged developers by offering financial incentives to invest in these conversion projects. More and more people were living downtown. The conversions needed to be done with green construction, incorporating natural materials with environmentally sound techniques. It is expected that many of the service industries will return to the downtown as the population increases.

Each time Judy greeted newcomers to the city, she was excited to be the person who welcomed them to her city and their new life.

The electric car pulled into the driveway.

"Manuel, put a leash on Charlie," said Jose.

They all exited the vehicle. It was nighttime, much later than they expected to reach their destination. Judy appeared from the front door of the older bungalow located in a well-kept southeast neighbourhood of houses built in the early 60s.

"Hello, folks, welcome to Regina. I hope your trip was okay."

Freda answered, "It was fine. We had a wait at the border, but you had told us that would happen. We're so happy to finally be here."

"I'll give you a quick tour of the house and then get out of your hair. You must be tired. Use your GPS to find my office tomorrow. I'll provide you with the information you need to settle tomorrow. I bought a few things, like coffee and buns for the morning. There's information on the kitchen counter about grocery shopping nearby. If you've not eaten supper yet, you can order Chinese or pizza and they'll deliver," said Judy.

Freda was pleased with the house. The furnishings were of good quality and tasteful. Beds and mattresses were newer. They were paying $3,000 a month for the furnished home. They'd been told that rental properties were difficult to come by, but the University of Regina had helped them by renting this place. Jose was being paid $5,000 a month, so there wouldn't be a lot left over after the rent and taxes. But they have $300,000 in US dollars, almost $400,000 Canadian. Invested, it will help them with their expenses. Freda cannot work. Immigration has not yet granted her a work permit. Once she is able to work, they hope to buy their own place.

Judy gave them their keys and departed. She left them to unpack what they need and get some rest.

~

Regina Welcomes You was located in an older, two-story brick building downtown on Smith Street. Jose dropped Freda and the children at the building entrance and drove around looking for parking. He found a spot across from the library next to Regina's Victoria downtown park. As he walked back to Smith Street, he noted how many of the buildings had been updated to be more environmentally friendly. He was familiar with the newer building codes that addressed climate change. When water restrictions were introduced in La Cruces, he had attended the sessions informing residents about the newer cleaner codes that were being introduced. Regina was way ahead of La Cruces.

After entering the building, he saw Judy and Freda in a children's area. They were watching Victoria and Manuel playing with a girl about Victoria's age. The children were all speaking in Spanish.

"Good morning, Jose," said Judy.

"And good morning to you. Who is the young girl?" He asked Judy.

"Her name is Camila. Did you hear about the terrible deaths of a Central American family in southern Saskatchewan about three months ago?"

"Yep, sad."

"Camila is the only surviving family member. She's under the protection of our Child Protection Services. They could not locate where she's from to determine if relatives can be found so they can repatriate her. Some days, Social Services has us look after her in the daytime. She plays with other children who come in with their parents. She has not learned much English yet."

Freda looked interestingly at the little girl. Judy picked up on that.

"Freda, Social Services has a difficult time finding foster parents. Camila has been difficult to place because of language difficulties. They pay foster parents about a $1,000 a month and a stipend for extra child development costs. You might qualify even though you just arrived. Of course, they do serious vetting. But you'd be perfect foster parents, since she can communicate with you and socialize in a Spanish environment.

"She has had unimaginable trauma, so it wouldn't be easy. She is receiving some counselling."

Freda looked at Jose, who wouldn't return her look. He was afraid she'd say yes.

Jose responded, "Judy, we'll talk about it."

They left the children playing and went to Judy's office.

Judy advised them that her organization assists immigrants in linking them to medical services, school, housing, banking, employment if needed, and English language training, if needed.

Judy told Jose and Freda that housing has been very difficult to find for immigrant newcomers to the city. The booming green economy has attracted migration to Saskatchewan from other provinces. This has created a high demand for rental properties and a hot housing market. Homes sell within 3 days on the market. Bidding is pushing list prices up. New home builds are not keeping up to demand.

"Freda and Jose, if it weren't for your ability to prove that you are able to pay with the University of Regina vouching for you, you might not be in such a nice place."

Freda grabbed Jose's hand and held it tight. It is a sign of her relief that they have their place.

Judy continued, "I'm recommending that you buy a three-month health care insurance policy today. There is an insurance agent we work with whose office is just down the street. It will cost you $3,000 for three months, but it is a onetime expense and; you don't want to have any health issues without coverage in these three months. After a three month wait, you'll be eligible for our universal health care plan.

"I'm going to take you to Sask Health after you purchase the private insurance. There, you will register for the public health plan. Then, I'm going to take you to a bank where you can sort your money affairs out.

"After that, we will see each other on a need-to basis. This pamphlet will inform you about everything you need to do and where you can do it. Your utilities are set up. The University did that for you. You will need a Saskatchewan driver's license and plates for your car. This agency is called Saskatchewan Government Insurance. You will be issued a driver's license from them, but private insurance vendors issue your plates and public insurance.

"Any questions?"

Freda answered, "It's a lot of information. We'll work our way through it all and get back to you if we get stuck on anything. And Jose and I will let you know about our decision concerning Camila."

Jose knows what that decision will be. Freda is not the kind to say no to a little girl in need.

20

MR. BIG

REGINA, SASKATCHEWAN

Peter Hamilton left the courthouse on Victoria Avenue a free man after a Judge ruled there was not enough evidence to show he was complicit in the killing of the Central American family or that he had obstructed justice.

TV cameras filming his exit from the courtroom for the evening broadcasts followed him to his car. He kept his eyes straight ahead while walking to a waiting cab.

He had tossed the revolver when the police raided the North Central home. The pistol had had the serial number filed down. When the police discovered it in the house, they could not trace it to him.

The home was a drug den. He had figured that's where he would find Robert. His youngest had always been the dumbest of his boys, and a druggy to boot.

The police raid happened so quickly that Hamilton had no time to speak with Robert. It wouldn't have mattered. The idiot was stoned.

Prior to his hearing that morning, the Judge had ordered Robert to be detained on murder charges. The wrist band, in his opinion, was compelling physical evidence.

Hamilton hired a well-known Regina lawyer for his son. The lawyer had a reputation for being sleazy. Sleazy is what he wanted. Hamilton was prepared to give up Robert to ensure he did not implicate his two older brothers. Hamilton wants the lawyer to cut a deal with the prosecutor, and for Robert to plead guilty on all three murder charges.

The cab drove Hamilton to the Regina Police compound, where he recovered his Cadillac SUV and headed for Willow Bunch.

∼

CORPORAL JENNINGS DROVE to Regina to meet with Sergeant Dagenais of the RCMP's major crimes unit. The Sergeant had asked him to come up from Coronach and remain in Regina for a few nights. Dagenais was impressed with Jennings's work on the Big Muddy murders.

Jennings' superior had approved his temporary absence from the detachment.

Dagenais is organizing a Mr. Big sting. An undercover RCMP officer is going to be Robert Hamilton's cellmate at the Regina Corrections Detention Centre.

The new cellmate will impersonate a high-ranking member of a biker gang, a far more notorious group than the Ole Boys. The new cellmate is from Calgary, where the biker gang named Razor's Edge operates. His rap sheet is extensive. He's being held for the attempted murder of a Regina biker gang member. The story line is that a local biker hassles the Razor's Edge member over a woman he has been fondling at a local bar. The local biker claims that the woman is his friend's old lady. A fight breaks out and the Calgary biker carves up the local biker really bad.

After explaining the narrative, Dagenais offered Lyle the opportunity to serve as the undercover case manager. If he accepts, he'll liaise with the undercover and organize police action when valuable information comes out.

Lyle agreed right away.

Dagenais said, "Robert Hamilton has been doing lots of opioids since the murders. He is addicted. We're going to make sure he has access to opioids in jail. His lawyer is a two-faced son of a bitch. We have control over him. Some years back, he embezzled some money. We paid off the man he had cheated and did not press charges. Since then, he has been helping us out from time to time.

"Robert's father will not pay for his son's habit. But we will. His lawyer will provide the money under the guise that the lawyer was over-billing the old man and passing some of the extra money on to Robert to help him buy drugs inside. Corrections officers will turn a blind eye to Robert's drug purchases.

"Our undercover will impress the much younger Robert by telling him he's a kingpin of the Razor's Edge biker gang. He will tell Robert he almost beat a local biker to death.

"After a short while, the source of Robert's lifeline will cease. His new cellmate will offer to assist him get off drugs. The Razor's Edge bikers trade in drugs, but members may not be users.

"Of course, the new cellmate wants Robert to trust him and confide in him."

Dagenais and Jennings meet again the next day to discuss the case further. Dagenais has a more permanent posting in the Major Crimes Unit for Lyle, which starts with being the Mr. Big case manager.

"It's not a promotion, Lyle. Your turn will come for that. What I'm offering you is a move to Regina to join me in the Major Crimes Unit," said Sergeant Dagenais.

"I'll take it," an excited Corporal Jennings responded.

"Okay, now, I want you to meet one of our best undercover Mounties."

Dagenais lifted his desk phone and spoke into it, "Please send in Lorne Wright."

A long-haired, unshaven young man in blue jeans and a dirty sweatshirt entered Dagenais's office. The man had an oniony smell about him.

"Corporal Jennings, meet Corporal Lorne Wright. Lorne is our covert undercover operative. In a few days, they will jail him for almost beating a local gang biker to death."

The two men shake hands.

∽

LYLE SAT ALONE in his hotel room drinking a beer. He was wearing civies. *Wow,* he thought, *criminal investigations are what I've dreamed of doing.* Now that it was happening, would that change his disintegrating marriage? There had been no contact between them since her hasty exit after their argument. For him, his job was his priority. Did he love her? Did she love him? The lack of communication over the last three months spoke volumes.

Right from the beginning, he should have realized she would not like the effects her husband's job would have on her. They'd rushed into their marriage. It's on him, he admitted to himself. He could have impressed on her more that there would be rural town postings, that she would be alone a lot, that she would worry whether he would come home from a shift, that there were regular night shifts, that there would be rental housing challenges in smaller towns, etc. But they fell in love, and passion won out over reason.

The biggest spousal challenge was having to forgo career opportunities. Jobs using a spouse's skills and education were difficult to find in many of the postings. And if, by chance, the spouse did get a job, he or she would have to quit when a new posting came through and start the job search again.

No, he said to himself, it's over. Lyle decided he would see a lawyer and file for divorce.

∼

Corporal Lorne Wright entered the cell. He said nothing to his new cellmate. He went over to the lower bunk, picked up the other fella's bedroll, and threw it on the top bunk.

"What the fuck?" griped Robert Hamilton, agitation covering his baby face. "That's my bed, you prick."

The unkempt, rugged man looked at Hamilton and said, "Fuck off, kid. You want to take it back?" Wright quickly established that he was the alpha dog in this cell.

And that was all that was said between them during the first day and night.

The next morning, a contrite Hamilton greeted his cell mate. No answer, only silence from the other man, which unnerved Hamilton. He popped an opioid. He was running out of his supply. It was his last one. The fellow in the yard who had been supplying him was no longer showing up.

By the afternoon, Hamilton was trembling and rubbing his arms. He was anxious. Sweat was running down his face and the back of his neck. He was pacing in the small cell.

Wright told him to relax. Hamilton could not.

"Kid, are you needing a hit?" asked Wright.

"Yeah, it's hard to get lately, especially since they don't let me mix a lot with the general population. They tell me I'm too young and pretty. I'm okay with that. I'm afraid of what could happen. You hear so much on the outside about what goes on inside a prison."

Wright smirked. "You bet. You're better off away from the perverts. Do you want me to protect you? Cost you; I do nothing for free. You have money or else you wouldn't be buying drugs."

Hamilton doesn't want to play his hand with this dangerous man. The guards have been protecting him. Why should he pay this guy? Or, is the guy saying, "Pay him or he'll do something to him?" Hamilton wishes the man had never showed up.

"Maybe ... I'll think it over. I had an easy time buying in the yard when I was being let out for fresh air. There was this other guy in the yard who told me he was also being protected from the main population. But the guy's not showing up anymore."

"Hmm, how do you pay?" asked Wright.

"Why would I tell you?"

"Because you're a user whose supply has been cut off. In a few hours, you'll be whining for me to help you. By midnight, you'll want to die. Look, kid, I'm all you got right now."

"My lawyer is bringing money for me." Hamilton reached into his pillow and drew out a few hundred dollars.

"You give me some of that, and I'll get you something to help. My gang sees drug usage as a weakness. Our philosophy is that we have control over ourselves. Drugs don't weaken us, women don't own us, and governments don't order us; we are independent beings, our body, our sanctuary and our freedom sacred."

"No, I need opioids."

"Look, kid, it's called buprennorphine. It's an opioid. It's acts more slowly in your body. You can go through withdrawal easier using it," said Wright.

"No, I'm gonna save my dough to buy the genuine stuff," said Hamilton.

"Do the fuck what you want, kid. I'm not your mother."

Robert Hamilton's trembling and pain was soon accompanied by nausea and chills. By evening he was begging Wright for buprennorphine.

"It's $20 for a daily dose. You pay me an extra $100 a day to get it for you. I pay the guard an additional $100 a day. Can you continue to get money from that lawyer?"

Hamilton whimpered, "Yes, he's stealing from my dad and sharing that with me."

"It might take up to ten days to withdraw. Then after that, you'll pay me $50 a day for two weeks to keep you from going over the deep end when you stop taking buprennorphine."

Hamilton was too needy to see he was being snaked by Wright.

"Okay, yeah, I can do that. When can you get the drug for me?"

"Give me $220 now," demanded Wright. Hamilton did as he was told.

"Guard, come here quick," yelled Wright.

The guard appeared. Wright whispered to him and gave him $120. Wright pocketed the $100 for himself.

The guard returned in a short time with a small pill container. He gave it to Wright, who turned it over to Hamilton. Within a half hour, Hamilton's condition and composure improved.

Robert Hamilton became suspicious. "How were you able to make that happen so easily?"

Wright was prepared with an answer. "Kid, have you heard of the Alberta gang called the Razor's Edge?"

"Yeah, I'd be pretty stupid not to have. They control drugs and weapon trafficking and auto theft in Alberta. Tough guys who will kill if needed," said Hamilton.

"Well, I'm pretty high up in the gang. In fact, I'm a founding member. When I entered here after my arraignment, I arranged with friendly prison guards to look after me."

"No shit! I'm an Ole Boy, and I wasn't able to arrange things like that. And, we aren't into the type of shit you are. We buy weapons only for our members. Rarely do we raise money from crime. Membership and donations from like-minded folks keep us going. I'm sorry about disrespecting you when you first came."

"Kid, the first thing you gotta know in prison is your place. Otherwise, you'll get hurt inside. I'm not a nice guy, and I ain't helping you out of the goodness of my heart. Keep paying me, cause if it stops, then so does our blossoming friendship. Am I clear?"

Hamilton replied, "Yes, I get it. Don't worry."

For the next month, Wright helped his cellmate out and told him all about his gang and the type of guys they like to recruit. Hamilton took it all in, and being young and impressionable, asked if he could join them someday. Wright told him the gang needed guys like him who would kill if ordered to do so.

While all this was happening, Hamilton's lawyer showed up with the money. When he asked Hamilton what it was for, Hamilton just told him it was for protection against the bad guys. He never mentioned Wright.

As time passed, Hamilton talked more and more about what he was prepared to do. Then one day, at Wright's urging, he spilt how he and his brothers murdered the Central American family. He also told Wright where his brothers were.

Shortly afterward, a guard came to the cell and told Wright to pack his things. He was being transferred to Calgary to face charges there.

∼

REGINA HAS an encampment that houses the homeless. There are shelters made of disposed or stolen building materials, tents, and some small mobile trailers. Many of the people in the encampment have jobs. People are homeless because there's nowhere else for them to stay. There is an area in the far corner of the encampment occupied by drug addicts and the mentally ill.

Corporal Wright returned to the encampment once he was released from jail. He always has to be a pretender. Two years earlier, he had divorced himself from a normal cop's life. Single, ambitious, and adventurous and in his mid-thirties, he took up the role of an undercover operative with enthusiasm. He relished the work he has done to put bad people behind bars.

Armed only with multiple fake identifications, he uses his acting skills to get by. He never carries a gun.

Soon, the gig will be up. He's up for a promotion, and they will assign him to another area of work.

Jennings met him on a really hot day near the encampment.

"Which mansion is yours, Lorne?" asked Lyle.

"I'm over with the group that is most in need. I've a persona to maintain."

"What do you have for me?"

"Who did what and the circumstances The kid started the killing when he panicked after the young victim attacked him." Wright filled Jennings in on the rest of the details.

Wright said to Jennings, "He's impressionable, and his father and older brothers have not been outstanding role models. I feel for him and hope he's only charged with manslaughter. The other two murdered the others with intent."

Wright passed Lyle the information on the location of the two brothers. Next the police will play one brother against the other.

21

TORNADO

WILLISTON, NORTH DAKOTA

Mark and Mandy moved into a furnished rental farmhouse just north of Williston, North Dakota. The rent was $1,500 a month, a lot less than it would've been in Williston. Mark found a warehouse job right away that paid $20 an hour.

Mandy drives him to work every day. She does the shopping for groceries and household needs. After a short time, she also found a job as a server at Applebees in Williston.

There were far fewer black people in North Dakota than in the southern States. People in the area seemed to be respectful sorts. At least, that had been their experience.

Mandy shared with her dad what she learned about the folks from the area.

"You know, dad, I've learned at Applebees that you don't tell North Dakotans that life is better elsewhere or complain that stores are closed on Sundays. Nor do you look for pity or else they'll lose respect for you. It seems they expect people to suffer a bit in life."

Chuckling, Mark replied to his daughter, "Black people from the south would have no problem fitting that criteria."

Mandy told her dad about some other North Dakota characteristics she had discovered.

"If someone helps you out, say thank you, but don't get all flowery. Show up if you say you will, and if you can't, let them know in advance and be regretful the next time you're talking to them. Rural people are more conservative than city folks. And winter is like Siberia."

Mark stared at his beautiful daughter. She was maturing well enough without a mother? But Mark is not naive. He knows she needs a woman's influence. He had seen how quickly she and Freda had bonded.

They are months, maybe years, away from receiving approval to settle in Canada. He likes Williston. The city's agricultural industries and oil and gas businesses provide a strong local economy. Maybe he should just try to get a football coaching job here, and Mandy could attend college here as well.

The oil and gas production did cause him some concern. It was causing water contamination, and fracking was causing quaking in the area. But it was not a significant issue for him. His decision to remain would depend on how safe they felt and whether he could get better employment. The environment had not been his reason for leaving Colorado.

∼

HE WAS DRIVING the company truck back from Bismarck with supplies for the warehouse and started listening to a podcast about global warming and its effects. The podcast was produced by a guy named Allan Walker.

Walker was interviewing a renowned environmental scientist, Doctor Peter Wong. Jackson had never heard of him before, but as he listened, he found that the topic was quite interesting. Wong was speaking about the earth's warming.

"As the earth continues to heat up due to man-made climate change, record temperatures are occurring throughout our world. The past five years have been earth's hottest years ever. Earth is reaching a tipping point where the warming trend cannot be reversed. Greenhouse gas emission must be reduced now."

Mark Jackson looked up at the sky. There were dark clouds moving fast overhead. Suddenly, a swirling, menacing black cloud appeared ahead. Huge lumps of hail hit his windshield, shattering the glass and sending pieces flying. An uprooted tree flew through the air toward his truck and crashed into the roof of the cab, crushing it. The truck was picked up and thrown into a field where it rolled over and over until it came to rest some 60 feet from the road.

∼

"Oh, honey, I'm so sorry. My God, how dreadful. Yes, we'll leave at once to get you," promised Freda.

Mandy had phoned to tell Freda that her dad had been killed that day in a tornado. She was beside herself with grief and did not know what she needed to do. She thought of Freda at once as the person she needed most beside her now.

From Regina, Saskatchewan, to Williston, North Dakota, is a three-hour drive. It was dark when Jose finally pulled into the farm house driveway. One of Mandy's girlfriends from Applebee's was with her.

Freda and Mandy held each other tightly. Mandy cried brokenly for her loss and Freda wept with her and for her.

Mandy's girlfriend brought Jose up to date on the details of the accident and where Jackson's body was being held.

The TV was on the sports network. A reporter was saying, "Former National Football League player Mark Jackson, a Rookie of the Year, whose career was cut short because of injury, has lost his life in a tornado in North Dakota. We would like to extend our condolences to his family.

"We don't know why he was in North Dakota. After he left football, we have heard little about him. Some initial reports show he coached a high school football team."

Jose turned off the TV and walked Mandy's girlfriend to her car.

Three days later, Mandy and her father's ashes accompanied the Kirks back to Regina. Freda looked forward to getting back to her children and Camila. Her family was growing.

22

POLITICAL CANDOUR
DIEFENBAKER LAKE, SASKATCHEWAN

Prime Minister Pauline Gervais flew to Regina from Ottawa in a government-owned Bombardier Challenger, an electric-powered jet. Julian, her Chief of Staff, and her security detail accompanied her.

Premier Rebecca Mahon, Sammy Nelson, and Mahon's security detail met them at the Regina International Airport.

The Prime Minister and Premier are meeting at the Hotel Saskatchewan with First Nation and Métis leaders from northern Saskatchewan. The issues to be discussed are related to the effects of global warming on the boreal forests and wildlife. Aboriginal leaders want more say in combatting climate change and the resources to do so.

They meet in a large meeting room. The agenda has one of the First Nations leaders speaking.

The speaker is a Tribal Chief of the Cree Nation. She read a statement. "Climate change has hurt our northern lands more than others in the Province. The forests are on fire. Our trees are infested with insects never before seen on our land. Hunting and fishing is not as plentiful as before. We want to be included in solving the problems.

"For centuries, we have maintained the health of our lands using the methods passed down by our forefathers. Our prevailing value is that we take from Mother Earth only what we need. It's our belief that governments, including our own, and the private sector, must embrace that sentiment. Capitalism, with its profit-driven goal, is resulting in too much take and not enough preservation. For many years, your economic system has poisoned our waters with chemicals from nearby industries and depleted the wildlife our people depend on for our food. Your farmers have used pesticides and insecticides that poison our water and wildlife.

"It is the non-indigenous people with capitalism as their creed that has brought on global warming. Our traditional way of life is being threatened once again."

The Métis spokesperson delivered a similar message.

The meeting resulted in all three parties reaffirming past agreements to partner in the fight against the global warming effects in northern Saskatchewan's aboriginal-held lands.

The Prime Minister showed a willingness to provide more funding to aboriginal people to combat climate change.

An entourage of political aides and RCMP security accompanied the Prime Minister and Premier to the shores of Diefenbaker Lake. The lake is a two-hour drive northwest of Regina. Once there, they met up with local politicians and area business people.

Today, the wind turbines are being turned on for the first time. The two billion dollar partnership between the private sector and the two governments already had multiple sales contracts with many western European countries to supply their energy needs with green hydrogen turned into ammonia. The return to investors would be substantial.

The investors have also funded upgrades to the harbour at Churchill, Manitoba, where tankers will ship containers of ammonia to buyers in Europe.

There are media people from across Canada at this event. Many local folks from the area are in attendance, along with cottagers who spend time at the lake during the summer months.

It is so hot you could fry an egg on the side walk. Dignitaries speak from a covered stage. Dressed in formal clothing, the dignitaries swelter in the unrelenting heat.

After the ribbon-cutting, the two government leaders headed to a cabin on the north shore of the lake. Sammy's hometown of Outlook is nearby. She broke off from the group to visit her mother at the Outlook Care Home.

She had arranged for the use of the cabin for one night for herself and three other government officials. They had towed in fifth wheelers for the security details and political aides to use.

∼

"Hi mom, are you being well-cared for here?" asked Sammy.

Her mother's eyes sparkled with joy when she heard her daughter's voice; she turned in her wheelchair to see her.

"Sammy, my baby, oh my baby," tears fell from her eyes.

Sammy went to her mother and hugged her close.

"Where is Rebecca?"

"Oh mom, she's busy being premier of our province. She's hosting the Prime Minister at a cabin on the lake."

"How are the two of getting along? You two have been together for some time now."

"Mom, I'm not the monogamous sort. It's part of that independence you taught me. Rebecca is clingy. It gets to me sometimes, and when it does, I cheat on her."

"Oh, Sammy. Why are you telling me this?" Her mother's smile had faded.

"I'm not sure. You're the only person I confide in. Maybe I just want to say it to someone before I tell Rebecca."

"You're thinking of telling her?"

"Mom, I'm not sure," Sammy sniffed the air and changed the subject. "It sure smells of urine and shit in here."

"My baby, you get used to it. It's not bad here. I'm looked after. It's cool in here when it's hot outside and warm when it's cold. The food is okay. And it's the only option I have."

Sammy looked at her mom. She had never considered having her mother live with her. Sammy was a busy person and, even though she loved her mother dearly, she was not the nurturing sort. Sammy stayed an hour visiting and then joined the others at the cabin.

∼

GERVAIS AND MAHON have been friends since the first time they met. Their ideas and ambitions align. They both had wanted this one night to get away for a bit of R and R. The rigours of politics was exhausting.

Inside the luxurious four-bedroom cabin, Sammy showed the others the well-stocked bar. No one hesitated. They all poured themselves a robust drink.

Pizza ordered from Outlook arrived. They drank wine with their food. It relaxed them and loosened up their conversation.

Premier Mahon pulled a joint out of her purse. The others laughed. They shared the joint among the four of them.

Julian, the only male present, went to the bar and grabbed a bottle of very good bourbon and four glasses.

"Julian, if I ever wanted a husband, I'd marry you," said Gervais.

"Pauline, I'm married already."

"Oh, and that too," she chuckled.

Gervais never married because she never wanted to divide her loyalties. She had grown up in Montreal. From an early age, she had wanted to change the world to make it a better place. She didn't know what that meant for her, but it was in her nature to join something that promoted a better life for others. She spoke both of Canada's official languages, English and French, and had a law degree from McGill University. Now in her mid-sixties, she was the Prime Minister of Canada with a majority government.

Mahon asked Gervais, "Are the threats on your life increasing on social media? Mine are."

Gervais rolled her eyes and replied, "I'm being told by the Canadian Security Intelligence Service (CSIS) that they are.

They tell me right-wing organizations are springing up all over this country as President Petry and the Patriots of America Party turn a blind eye to them in the United States. Financial help for our sprouting right wing movement has been flowing into Canada from the United States since the 2022 convoy occupation of Ottawa's downtown."

Mahon scrunched her face, "Have you heard about what happened at a library in Idaho? Five years ago, this library was named the number one small town library in the United States. A band of right-wing Christians entered the library with guns to remove the Hand Maid's Tale written by Margaret Atwood. They removed that book and others on their list. The local sheriff will not press charges because he agrees with their action."

The four of them yelled, "Oh fuck!"

"Do you know that Shit-for-Brains …" started Gervais.

Sammy asked, "Hmm, you mean Petry?"

"Yes, well Shit-for-Brains hangs up on me regularly when I won't do what he wants," said Gervais.

Sammy shouted over the others, "Bang the damn receiver on your desk when you're talking to him. The noise will make him deaf," she chortled. They all laughed.

"So this one time, he phoned me about our enhanced NATO Arctic security. He tells me that there are Inuit people working covertly with Russia and China to help them claim our Artic territory as theirs. He wants me to allow American CIA to operate in the area. So I start being passively aggressive. I don't use it very often, but he never listens to me except to make sure I'm agreeing with him. So I decide to play along."

Gervais paused. Between smoking weed and drinking, she could hardly hold back peals of uncontrollable laughter.

"Now, I call him Shit-for-Brains, but he's a brilliant manipulator and knows how to use lies and exaggerations to his advantage. He's also an expert in bullying. But he's also gullible. So, I ask him if his CIA agents speak any Inuit. He says, no, he doesn't think so. I tell him he could use our CSIS Inuit Language Training Institute to teach his agents the language. It's a four-year program. He says, but that's too long. So I say to him, wouldn't it be better if we just send our CSIS agents to the north? He agreed."

Mahon was laughing out loud, "You didn't?"

"I did. Petry is one of these people who has an idea a minute. He promotes it, then forgets about it because he's onto the next one. So, he's forgotten about the CIA station in our north or he thinks we have agents up there spying on our own countrymen."

As darkness falls, there is more banter among these important, responsible people who rarely let their hair down.

Sammy has more difficulty than the others engaging in small talk. She wants the others to pay attention to her. Her face hardens as her mood darkens.

"Ten years ago, the city of Las Vegas, New Mexico, not Nevada, but New Mexico, had twenty days of fresh water left.

"The state's largest wildfire ever scorched the hillsides. The fire burned over 340,000 acres. The monsoon season brought heavy rainfall that led to more disaster. The rainfall washed the charred debris into the region's water collection system. Officials scrambled to find other sources of water to prevent people from drinking the water that had cancer-causing particles flowing out of their faucets.

"One of the city's two reservoirs was filled with contaminated water that the filtration system could not handle. The mixed of carbon and chlorine in the water can cause it to be carcinogenic.

"Now the city could install another treatment system able to treat heavy sediment, but the government did not address the recurring forest fires from the ongoing droughts. And we all know, the droughts are the result of the greenhouse gas emissions. These types of incidents are popping up all over the southwest United States. For some parts of the United States, local conditions have already become too extreme, and it's too late to adapt. People are moving away; many, the poor, are moving to Canada."

Mahon was perturbed at her partner for putting an end to their fun and asked, "What's your point, Sammy?" Rebecca forced a smile. "Have another drink, smoke a joint, but don't fucking talk shop when we're taking a break from it."

"My point, dammit, my point, Rebecca, is that we Canadians need our friends to the south to work with us on relocation issues, plans and actions. We're drinking and laughing at the leader of the United States. I get it, he's not the person we want to work with, but we have to or else find officials there who will work with us."

Gervais, her interest perked, interjected, "Rebecca, please let Sammy continue."

Rebecca glowered at Sammy but withheld further comment.

Sammy continued, "It's just the beginning. Millions are moving north from South America, Central America, and Mexico to the United States border.

"People are entering the United States illegally.

"The Americans are being more diligent in hunting the illegals down, and deportation numbers are way up.

"Illegals, joined by poorer Americans, are making their way to our borders. And right now, Canada looks pretty good addressing global warming, but we are facing some of the same issues as other countries that we are already too late to address. That's because no man is an island. What happens elsewhere will have an impact here. And it's all happening sooner than later. Forecasts point to 2050 as a date when there will be places on earth that humans, because of heat, will not survive. Think about it, a new baby is born today and will only be 18 in 2050.

"Pauline, I think we must work with every country in the world. We need an international agreement on world migration. The idea here is to have all of us working together. You know, *We Are the World*. Sammy hums a few chords of the old song.

"The world needs to recognize that there will be places on earth that will no longer support life. That means we spend world income on helping people move and settle in cooler regions.

"In 2050, that might mean moving one-third of our world's population. There is plenty of available space to move people. The surface of Canada itself is 9.9 million square kilometres."

Gervais spoke, "Much of our northern land is rock and muskeg. It's not habitable."

Sammy replied smugly, "Pauline, you're looking at it through the wrong lens. I'm talking about possibilities; you're telling me why we can't."

Gervais smiled gently. "Oh, okay. Continue."

Sammy continued, "Our biggest challenge is our geopolitical organizations. Countries cry out we are already too full.

"I've said that people will move north. That's what's occurring now. As a general rule, people will need to move away from the equator, and from coastlines, small islands (which will shrink in size), and desert regions. Rainforests and woodlands are also places to avoid, due to increased fire risk. Populations are going to shift inland, towards lakes, higher elevations, and northern latitudes."

"Canada is the fifth largest economy on the planet. Our federal government can show world leadership on this. You must, in the same manner that our former Prime Minister Pearson did to bring about peace in the Middle East."

Premier Rebecca Mahon wanted to leave the serious discussion behind and return to the fun and laughter. She was perturbed at Sammy. "Why couldn't she turn off her vigilance once in a while? She was taking over the conversation."

"Sammy, that's enough of your seriousness. We've so little time in our busy lives to enjoy ourselves. Get another joint. You and Pauline can follow up on this another time." She inhaled on her joint.

Rebecca, stoned and her face flushed, blurted out, "If I'm a migrant looking for the best place to live, I'd fucking come here.

"Saskatchewan's future is untapped. At the beginning of the 20th century, predictions were that Saskatoon would someday be the Chicago of the north. This evening, influenced by some superb weed, I'm making that prediction.

Saskatoon in 50 years will be Canada's Chicago. Except, the city will be operated on new, cleaner types of energy."

Gervais laughed, "Winnipeg might have something to say about that."

"Pooh on that," crowed Mahon.

Sammy piped in again, "Around 2009, a wealthy Winnipeg man divested his interest in Winnipeg properties and bought up Saskatchewan farmland. He wanted to own something that would be in demand that China could not control. He felt that was agriculture and water. Saskatchewan was the place he chose. The man now owns 300,000 acres of the best farmland in the province. He improved that land by cleaning away dead trees and old farm equipment, and improving farming practices.

"Now while I'm not wholly in agreement with his use of fertilizer, I'm impressed by his desire to contribute to a growing global population and a growing world middle class that is demanding a protein-rich diet. He sees urbanization taking more farmland out of production and drought destroying more and more farmland. The war in eastern Europe has placed even more stress on the world's food supply. This man invested his money in Saskatchewan."

Gervais exclaimed, "What's your point?"

Sammy shouted out, "Saskatchewan is where it's fucking happening.

PART III

FALL 2032

23

WONG WALKS AMONG THE SPIRITS
REGINA, SASKATCHEWAN

Peter Hamilton's resources were dwindling. News of the charges against his three sons for the murder of those wetbacks sent his customers scurrying elsewhere. Some of his finest and longest-serving workers told him they could not work for him anymore. It didn't matter, he couldn't pay them all anyway.

The number of Ole Boys in his group had dwindled. They were all right with distrusting government and liberalism, but having the RCMP knock on their doors asking questions about the Big Muddy murders scared them. After all, they were just rural folks looking for a life away from the big cities.

With his business sliding and legal bills skyrocketing, Hamilton sold off his equipment. Damn boys, how could they have been so stupid? He had thought they had learned to think on their feet. Maybe, that no good mother of theirs was right, I controlled them too much. Fuck, what did she ever get right?

The RCMP van pulled up to the curb just outside the Regina courthouse.

Two constables got out, followed by the two handcuffed brothers. The brothers smiled for the camera.

At first Hamilton reasoned it might be a good idea to have one lawyer defend all three of his sons. The sleaze bag lawyer could have Robert plead to all five killings, and the other two could walk free. But Hamilton soon found out that when Robert learned his cellmate was a cop, he had the lawyer agree to a manslaughter plea right away. The lawyer had not even bothered to contact Hamilton to get his agreement.

So today, the two lawyers hired by Peter Hamilton will argue before the judge to have separate trials for each of his older boys. The lawyers both felt that separate trials with different jurors were in their best interests. Robert, after pleading guilty, will only have a sentencing hearing on the manslaughter charges. Hamilton had ceased paying Robert's legal fees.

The boys nodded to their father as they entered the courthouse. He nodded back.

Corporal Jennings was in the courtroom when the two brothers were brought in. He saw Peter Hamilton sitting further back. There's the man who turned his offspring into hateful human beings. There should be a crime for that. They should hold Peter Hamilton accountable for the carnage.

The judge ruled there would be separate trials. Afterwards, Jennings returned to his office. He was learning so much about detective work in the Major Crimes Unit, continuing to handle operatives and informers. Their information and leads are so critical in preventing and solving crimes. Jennings' work entails a lot of discreet meetings in dark and seedy places. No longer being with Anita, the timing of his work hours was a nonissue for him.

His divorce was moving along. It was easy. They had few assets to divide. It had been a brief marriage. The lawyers were handling matters, and he himself had no contact with Anita.

Lyle returned to his rental unit in downtown Regina after stopping at the office. There, he put on his jogging gear. Even though it was October; it was still like summer outside. He jogged down Scarth Street toward Wascana Park, a large urban park with a lake.

He ran around the lake. When he arrived at the legislative building, he sat down on a bench facing the water. Overhead, geese were flying in a V formation. Some of them will migrate south; others will stay around Regina for the winter. Regina just might have the worst goose problem in North America. That is what Lyle was thinking when an older man sat on the bench beside him.

Lyle looked at the well-dressed man and said hello. The older man's lower lip was trembling. His eyes stared out at the lake. His expression was downcast.

Lyle was concerned. "Sir, are you okay? Can I assist you in any way?"

The man returned the greeting then sat in silence. A few minutes passed, then he began to speak.

"When I grew up in Regina, October days were often cold, almost as if it were ready to snow. The past 15 years have been warmer, and on a day like today, you feel that summer is still with us. Our weather patterns are changing."

Lyle looked at the man with interest.

The man continued, as if he were thinking out loud and not really speaking to Lyle.

"And the weather pattern changes are the result of global warming. And the warming has also resulted in the disappearance of monarch butterflies." This time the older man lifted his head and spoke directly to Lyle. "When was the last time you saw one?"

Lyle couldn't say, and had never really thought about it. He told the man it was a while.

"The bee and bat populations are also nearly extinct. Do you know why you should know that?"

Lyle shook his head no.

"Because these three creatures are all pollinators. They pollinate fruits, vegetables and other plants that are sources of our food supply. We are losing some of our favourite foods. Apples, melons, cranberries, pumpkins, squash, broccoli, and almonds are at risk.

"Our meat diets also depend on these since animals eat plants dependent on pollination for renewal.

"Drought, forest fires, and severe weather have limited the pollinator's source of food, such as the milkweed."

Lyle asked again, "Sir, are you in some sort of distress?" It was the man's woeful appearance and flat tone that concerned him most.

Dr. Peter Wong replied, "Only in the sense that I'm old, with two habits that control my being and result in the same outcome. You see, I gamble and I have the habit of warning others about global warming. I'm a loser on both accounts."

Lyle had seen this type of despair before in drug addicts trying to kick the habit. They have a sense of hopelessness, no passion, and no joy. *This man was checking all the boxes*, he thought.

"Sir, would you like me to accompany you to the hospital?"

Wong stood up and smiled at Lyle, "Everything happens for a reason, young man. Please do not be concerned about an old man who sees more happiness in his future."

Lyle considered following him, then decided to just let him walk on. He could not force him to go to a hospital.

Lyle resumed his jog.

∼

Wong returned to his home. Once there he sat down at his desk and began to write letters.

The first letter was to the Saskatchewan Commander of the RCMP. The second was to the Director of the FBI. The third was to a former friend at CNN. The three letters read the same. They outlined Bill Larsen's plan to murder Dan Weber, alias Allan Walker. They provided Larsen's motive as well as a listing of recordings, emails, and correspondence implicating Larsen.

The fourth letter was more heartfelt. It was a letter to Allan Walker. In it, Wong told him that his old nemesis, Larsen, sent him to find Walker and confirm that Walker and Weber were one and the same.

He explained that he, Wong, was not evil and could not be complicit in another man's death. He told Walker that the RCMP will be at his door once they read Wong's letter to them. The RCMP will likely protect him from Larsen. Wong emphasized that Larsen will seek revenge on Walker.

Wong added, "I know that I am exposing you to the Canadian Immigration authorities and that you will no doubt be deported. But I feel certain the RCMP and FBI will arrange for you to enter the US witness protection program. Even the American President cannot learn where you will be located. There are risks for sure, but if I did not do what I have, you'd be dead by now. Please look after Judy. Larsen might come after her too."

Wong wrote that he was caught between a rock and a hard place. He told Walker he was weak but that he also had some of the decency his father had shown when he was alive. Wong indicated that he was looking forward to soon walking among the spirits with his father.

"I don't know if you've ever told Judy who you are. If not, I'm sorry for the consequences, whatever they may be.

"I firmly believe you would be dead by now if I had not taken this course of action.

"With regrets and sorrow, Peter."

On his walk to Wascana Lake later in the warm fall evening, Wong mailed the four letters.

At the lake, he stripped down to his underwear. He stood at the edge of the water and thought for a few minutes. Sadness weighing heavily on his features, he recalled a story his teacher told her grade 5 class. Many years ago, his teacher told the story about the fish hawk.

The young fish hawk saw a large salmon in the river. He skimmed over the water's surface and grabbed what he thought was a dead salmon. His claws dug deeply into the fish. The fish was alive and swam far below the surface, taking the fish hawk with it. The fish hawk could not loosen his claws, and the fish drowned him. An analogy to his life? Was gambling his large fish? Peter had grabbed the large fish years ago, had stuck his claws in deep, and now the fish will drag him into the lake.

Touching the water with his toe sent a shiver through him. It was freezing cold. He was sure hypothermia would set in by the time he swam to the middle of the lake. Otherwise, he would drown because he couldn't swim all that well. He waded into the water and took the plunge. As the freezing water enveloped his body, he fought the urge to escape by thinking of that fish pulling him under.

24

FALL ENCOUNTERS
REGINA, SASKATCHEWAN

Jose sat in the living room watching the Major League Baseball playoffs. He is projecting the game from his tablet onto a screen.

The Toronto Blue Jays are playing the Los Angeles Angels. Aging superstars lead both teams. The Jays have Vladimir Guerrero, Jr., and the Angels have Shohei Ohtani.

Freda, their two children, and Camila and Mandy join him. Jose looks at his new family. Everyone helps. They all get along so well.

Freda said, "Honey, wouldn't it be nice if we could find something all of us might enjoy?"

Poor Jose, this happens all the time. Of course, no one is going to shout out, "This is so unfair, poor Jose."

"Yes, dear, what do you have in mind?"

They end up watching some reality TV show called America's Got Talent, a show that has been around for over 20 years.

While they watch TV, Jose thinks about the past 6 months. So much has happened. Once, just four mouths to feed, there are now six. Mandy still grieves but has taken positive steps to move on. Judy, from Regina Welcomes You, has helped with the process that allows Mandy to remain in Canada.

Jose has the means to support Mandy, but she does not want to be a financial burden. She found a job at the same Tim Horton's that was going to hire her dad. She also attends grade 12 classes. Mandy pays some room and board, against Jose's and Freda's objections. With the funds she provides, they have started a savings account for her future.

Camilla is a more challenging situation. She has difficulty with the loss of her parents. Freda, Jose, and their two children show her a lot of love and attention. Speaking to her in Spanish has been helpful.

But it is Mandy who makes the biggest difference. Mandy and Camilla share a bedroom. On those nights when Camilla can be heard weeping in her bed, it is Mandy who slides into bed and consoles her. And Mandy has taken up the duty of teaching Camilla to learn English.

Freda remains up after everyone has gone to bed. She has her tablet and reads the local news. The headlines this fall night are:

Russia enters Peace Talks with Ukraine. This has Previously led to Failure

Rich Nations won't Fight Climate Change until More of their own Die

China Permits Taiwan People to Vote on Governor Representative for Beijing

United States Reports Thousands of Americans in the Southern Part of the Country Died of Heat Stroke this Past Summer. Most were Poorer Folks without A/C

Saskatchewan New Green Party Nationalizes all Lithium Mining, including Chinese Company

The three Hamiltons Charged in Immigrant Family's Death will have Separate Trials

Saskatchewan New Green Party Passes Legislation that will Require Farmers to Stop Using Fertilizers that Cause Greenhouse Gas by 2036

Renowned Environmentalist, Dr. Wong, Found Dead in Wascana Creek.

Freda reads all the news, then goes to bed. This is her routine.

MEANWHILE IN WASHINGTON, DC:

Bill Larsen heard the news of Wong's death and phoned President Harrison Petry. He is put on hold for some time.

Petry finally came on, "What's up, Bill?"

God made both men from the same cloth, both loud, arrogant, and belligerent. So for Larsen to be rude to the President of the United States and for the President to respond in the same manner was just natural for the two of them, two peas in a pod.

Larsen screamed into his phone about the shit storm about to hit him, and Petry screamed back that nothing can come his way.

They carry on like this for a few minutes before Larsen said, "Stop it in its tracks. Get the FBI Director to seal any letter that comes into them from Wong. Next phone that bleeding heart, liberal stomping bitch in Ottawa, and get her cooperation to have the RCMP do the same."

"Why would I do that, Bill? Haven't I already got a pardon for you?" asked the President.

"You will do that," fumed Larsen, "because my closet will be open with all my files about your corruption when the FBI comes to my door."

"Okay, you've made your point. I'll let you know what happens," responded Petry.

∽

Drew Cousins, FBI Director, is an honest man who'd love to curtail the President's and PAP's efforts to make the United States less democratic.

The FBI has been monitoring all of Larsen's landline calls. A federal judge approved it after the FBI provided evidence that Larsen had been liaising with unfriendly foreign governments after his release from jail. The FBI considered Larsen (and the President of the United States) a threat to national security. The FBI could never monitor their own President's calls, but this call from Larsen's landline opened up the opportunity to record the President's deviant behaviour. So when Cousins received the summons to the White House, he already knew what it was about.

"Mr. President, what is it you actually want me to do?" quipped Cousins.

"Do your fucking job," yelled the President.

"But, sir," Cousins paused and cleared his throat, "We have no letter that I know of. They gave it perhaps to one of my field agents. We receive thousands of tips monthly. There would have been no reason for it to reach my desk," said Cousins emphatically.

The President was getting exasperated. He would like to fire this guy, but when the Director is hired, it's for a 10-year term. Oh yes, he had the authority, but there would be too much political and media blowback. It would not be worth it.

"Now listen, this is an order. Track that letter down and have it in my office by the morning," demanded the President.

"Yes Mr. President."

Cousins smiled as he left the oval office. He does not leak things to the press, but he has someone at a lower level who did just that, earlier in the day. By tomorrow morning, the letter will have circulated among most media outlets.

In Ottawa, Ontario:

"Madam Prime Minister, the President is on the phone wishing to speak to you. Should I put him through?"

"Just give me a minute." She reread the RCMP briefing note about Bill Larsen's death threats against a Regina podcaster.

"Okay, I'll take it now."

The President's loud, annoying voice traveled through the receiver. Pauline Gervais held the phone away from her ear. What she can understand is that he has a matter of national security, and he needs her help,

"Yes Harrison, please tell me." She does not want to alert him that she already knows what it is about.

The President tells her that there is an American citizen named Dan Weber who is living in Regina under the alias Allan Walker. This person is under suspicion of seditious acts against the American government. He is doing it with his anti-American podcasts.

"Mr. President, I tune into his very informative free speech podcasts about threats to democracy in the United States and about serious world threats like global warming. You really can't be serious?" stated the Prime Minister of Canada.

Petry is a serial liar. He is also as phoney as baloney. He paused, then lowered his voice as if he were about to share some top-secret information.

"Pauline, this has to be kept between you and me. Promise me."

"Sure Harrison, do tell.

"One of our intelligence officers gave this guy Dan Weber top secret documents before he fled our country. He then illegally entered your country with them. Later, our intelligence agents have pictures of him meeting with Chinese people and passing on the documents. The intelligence officer who gave him the documents has been detained. He has divulged that Walker is his accomplice. You must help us bring this guy in."

"Absolutely Harrison. I will have my border security agents apprehend him at once. We will put him in detention until we issue a removal order. He'll most likely lawyer up. The immigration lawyer will advise him to fight deportation. All of this will take time, and because Allan Walker is a bit of a Canadian celebrity, it will no doubt become public."

The President suspected she was playing games with him.

"Listen Pauline, cut the shit. What you do with him doesn't matter to me. I want you to destroy a letter that I'm certain the late Doctor Peter Wong wrote to a senior RCMP officer. You should intercept it and destroy it. Let that clown Walker continue his broadcasts as if nothing has happened. You can have him. I want that letter destroyed, you hear," shouted the President of the United States as if Gervais were required to accede to his demands.

"Harrison, Canada is a democratic sovereign country with laws. I can't be seen as above our laws. Mr. Walker will be detained and deported. The United States is a democratic country with laws, so when Mr. Weber is turned over to the United States, he will have all his rights as one of your citizens.

"The letter, if one exists, is probably in the hands of one of our investigators at our Major Crimes Unit in Regina. The ball will already be rolling on this."

Prime Minister Pauline Gervais laughed when she heard the explosion of wrath and the click of the phone at the other end.

In Regina, Saskatchewan:

Sergeant Dagenais and Corporal Jennings were sitting in the Walker's living room with Allan and Judy. Allan shared the letter he received in the mail that morning from Peter Wong. The detectives had informed them about Wong's death.

Dagenais told Walker about the letter received at the RCMP division office that morning. "It has been assigned to me and Corporal Jennings."

Judy advised that she was aware of Allan's real identity. They do not have secrets between them.

Allan advised the officers that, as an investigative reporter with CNN, he had uncovered crimes committed by Bill Larsen that resulted in the man's conviction and incarceration. Under threat from Larsen, he had fled Washington and came to Canada with a new identity.

Dagenais told Walker he was not taking him into custody. "That's our Border Security officers' job. They will not need a warrant to arrest you."

"Sergeant Dagenais, is it possible to hold off 24 hours before informing them? I have an interview tomorrow with a man who is a danger to our planet. I want to expose his lies about climate change."

"I've mistakenly placed an outgoing document into my in basket from time to time," responded Dagenais. "Please do not breach my trust and make me have to track you down."

"I promise, and thank you," replied Walker.

Outside, Jennings told Dagenais, "I met Dr. Wong just before he drowned himself. I thought he was distraught and offered to accompany him to the hospital. He got up and walked off. Maybe I should have done more?"

Dagenais replied, "He had decided his death was worth more to humankind than his life."

25

FAKE SCIENCE
REGINA, SASKATCHEWAN

Walker was interviewing Dr. Alex DeJong using Zoom.

DeJong is a geography professor at the University of Pittsburg. It is well known that he receives financial support from the coal industry. He readily accepts large grants for environmental research. His research always favours continuing the use of fossil fuels for energy. He points to bogus data and uses fear of change as his modus operandi.

Walker did not introduce the man by citing any accolades. Instead, he introduced him as a man whose ideas are controversial and divisive.

The professor started the discussion by suggesting fossil fuels are needed and do in fact make the world more habitable for humans.

"Professor, there are out-of-control wildfires throughout the world. Ash is falling into bodies of water, resulting in the poisoning of our drinking water. Floods, hurricanes, drought, and deforestation are causing mass migration from the affected regions. Tell me how that is good for humankind? How can you disagree with 95 percent of your colleagues that global warming is a threat to humankind?"

Smugly, the professor retorted, "It's obvious that you are one of the fear-mongering members of social media who pervade our society today."

"Professor, you are someone who elevates fringe research funded by the fossil fuel industry. You're a threat to the world's food and water security. And you call me a fear monger."

"I'm perfectly comfortable telling my critics that the climate has always changed. Powerful and complex, natural forces cause variable weather," countered DeJong. "No amount of effort to stabilize the climate might be successful. It's a waste of valuable resources. God has gifted us with energy like coal, oil, and gas. To think by not using them that man can change what's naturally occurring is nonsense." DeJong's tone exuded his sense of superiority.

"That is crazy thinking. That's what I say to my critics. President Petry is appointing me to a senior position in government environmental research and policy development. Shouldn't his trust in my views placate my adversaries?"

Walker took control of the interview at that point. He read emails submitted to him by the most renowned scientists from around the world. They attacked DeJong's lack of integrity and referred to his science as the science of self-interest.

DeJong discontinued the Zoom call in a huff. Walker hoped his audience saw through DeJong's deception and false narrative.

"THE BUSINESS SIDE of the podcast will remain in Regina. I'll podcast from the safe house," Allan said to Judy.

The FBI had reached out to Walker about ensuring his safety upon his return to the States. They had arrested Bill Larsen. International news media told the story around the world. The New York Times' headline was, *Time for the USA to Return to a Land of Laws*.

"Judy, my love, I'll be protected in an unknown location. The FBI won't even tell me where I'm going. Word is circulating that the House of Representatives, led by the minority Democrats, is drafting Letters of Impeachment. Hopefully that will end the lout's term early. Larsen is in jail. Bail is unlikely.

"The Canadian government has told me I can apply for legal immigration in a year's time. Then I will come back here."

"Dr. Wong died to protect you, Allan," murmured Judy.

"My God, he must have struggled so much. That's why he refused our invitations. I understand the Regina Chinese community is arranging for his internment at the cemetery where his father lies. Judy, I hope you'll attend."

"It's on my schedule," she replied.

The agent from Canada Border Security arrived for Walker.

"Mr. Weber, please come with me."

Walker, who goes by the name Weber again, got into an electric vehicle to be driven to a border crossing and handed over to the custody of the FBI.

∼

THE BURIAL SERVICE was sparsely attended. Wong had cut ties with Regina years earlier. An Oxford colleague flew over to attend. He provided a short eulogy. People gathered at the Chinese Community Association Hall for a small lunch. For a man who exposed so much political corruption and who spent much of his professional career warning people about global warming, it was an under-attended affair.

Judy attended the service and lunch.

∼

In Ottawa, Ontario:

President Harrison Petry used the tactic of sending word through a third party to the Prime Minister of Canada that there would be a cost to slighting him.

"Joe, tell our leftist neighbour that her *taking the high road* may be consequential to Canada and to her, but he would do what he could to prevent it."

The message reached Prime Minister Pauline Gervais. She understood his threat, but she was unconcerned. She believes he will be a yesterday person very soon.

CSIS informed her that there was a peaceful underground pro-democracy movement in the United States. The movement had some pretty powerful members in it, including the Director of the FBI. The movement's goal was to use the legal system to bring Petry to justice. Their motto was *No one is above the law*.

26

CANADA'S THANKSGIVING
REGINA, SASKATCHEWAN

Judy missed Allan. To combat her melancholy, she threw herself into her work at Regina Welcomes You. This year, she volunteered to coordinate a Canadian Thanksgiving celebration at the building owned by the Regina Exhibition Association Limited (REAL) to be held on Monday, October 11, 2032.

She is aided by volunteers from all immigration services in Regina and expects that the event will draw nearly five thousand immigrants.

Judy thought about the changes in immigration trends. Ten years ago, most immigrants settled in Montreal, Toronto and Vancouver. Currently, prairie cities were receiving a higher percentage of immigrants than in 2022.

Ten years ago, 62 percent of immigrants were Asian and 10 percent were from Europe. But those figures have changed.

Because of the ongoing fighting in eastern Europe, 20 percent of the 2031 immigrants were born in Europe; because of droughts and wars, 15 percent were born in the Middle East; and because of climate change, 20 percent were born in the United States or originated from the southern United States.

Asian-born immigrants still gravitate mainly to Montreal, Calgary, Edmonton, Vancouver, and Toronto because those cities have higher populations of Asian Canadians and the Asian culture is well established. She calculates that of the 8,000 immigrants arriving annually in Regina, 50 percent are from the area south of Saskatchewan.

She had just read that 30 percent of all Canadian residents were born outside of the country.

For many immigrants, it will be their first Canadian Thanksgiving.

She rented one of the newer buildings at REAL that could accommodate five thousand people. An executive management team was formed, and committees were established to oversee food, entertainment, and children's activities.

Freda volunteered to be on the food committee. The committee organized food booths for different types of food to be sold representing the cultures of the new immigrants to Regina. Freda wanted to ensure that a Tex-Mex booth was going to be there. She felt that was the food that most represented her background. She learned that there was fabulous

Mexican food restaurant in Vibank, Saskatchewan. At Freda's urging, the owner was setting up a booth.

∼

ON MONDAY, October 11, 2032, over five thousand immigrants gathered at the building for the Canadian Thanksgiving celebration. They dressed mostly in their cultural attire. It was a magnificent sight to see. This was diversity at its finest.

On the stage, children in costumes danced to music from all over the world.

People lined up at food booths eager to try the different foods.

Freda watched Camila, Victoria, and Manuel enjoying the children's activities. Jose was having a beer with some men at a table across the hall from her.

"Freda, gosh, I'm so happy to bump into you," said Judy.

Freda smiled, stood, and hugged Judy.

"This is great, Judy! You pulled it off. But, why am I not surprised? So many of us owe you and Regina Welcomes You so much."

A gracious Judy thanked Freda and asked, "How is Camila doing?"

"She doesn't express herself easily, and she frequently cries in the night. She lets Mandy soothe her. I think they find comfort in each other. Camilla's English is getting better. She attends school, and the teacher tells me she is very bright. She makes friends easily. She's part of my family now. Mandy is too. I love them both."

Freda asked Judy, "Do you know that man with the cowboy hat staring at you?" When Judy turned to look, the man had disappeared.

"No, Freda, I don't know any man who wears a cowboy hat."

Mr. Larsen had sent his orders; kill Weber's girlfriend. If Larsen couldn't get at Weber, then his revenge would have to be in another form.

The hitman mingled with the crowd. A woman talking to his target had looked curiously his way. He dropped back out of sight. He'd bide his time until this was over. Then, outside in the parking lot, he'd make his move.

Jose sipped on his beer. He was listening to a man from Jhansi, India, talk about the heat there. Weather, on the prairies, was the number one topic of conversation. Even the newest arrivals have taken it up.

The Indian man said, "People here are complaining about how hot it gets during the summer. Where I'm from, it's scorching hot. It gets to 50C from time to time."

Another man, dressed in an andura (white gown), from somewhere in northern Africa, spoke up. "Do you recall that heat burst in August? I think it was August 15th. Temperatures skyrocketed during the pre-dawn hours. Temperatures were hovering around 20C, then in an hour they'd risen to 32C. That type of heat rise is rare. I found this on the Weather Network platform."

The man read from his smart phone. "A heat burst is associated with thunderstorms that transfer warmer temperatures higher in the atmosphere down towards the Earth's surface, bringing gusty winds.

"The air is less dense in the upper atmosphere, but when it sinks, air pressure increases. The pocket of air compresses, causing the temperature to rise. An anomalous air mass remains if this air parcel doesn't mix with the surrounding air, which is likely what occurred in Regina.

"Typically, we see heat bursts at night because the ground cools off quicker than the air in the upper atmosphere. A collapsing thunderstorm pushes air towards the dry surface, and often the precipitation can evaporate before reaching the ground."

The man stopped reading and told the others, "The heavy wind that followed the heat burst blew our roof right off. I have experienced Sarahan Desert dust storms. The wind that morning that blew our roof off was as strong as any I've experienced."

"Yes," many of them piped in. "Regina is a windy city."

Jose said, "We have winds in New Mexico, where I'm from, like those Saharan dust storms. They come more frequently now. My wife tells me it's climate change."

The men spent the next two hours sipping beer and talking about the weather.

∽

THE EVENT ENDED at 8 PM. Judy remained behind on cleanup duty. It was 10 PM, when she left the building and walked to her car in the dark. She sensed that someone was following her. Then suddenly a burst of spotlights changed the dark parking lot into day. Voices barked out, "Don't move! Down on the ground!"

Judy turned toward the commotion. She saw a man, wearing a cowboy hat, being put in handcuffs and led to a police vehicle.

A man holding a police badge approached Judy and said, "We have things in hand, ma'am. My name is Corporal Jennings. I'm with the RCMP Major Crimes unit."

Judy, shock showing on her face, cried out, "What the fuck is happening?"

Jennings advised her that Bill Larsen wanted his revenge and had hired this man to hurt her.

"You might've warned me," said an incredulous Judy.

"You were always safe. We've had men watching out for you since we first learned of his plans," Jennings told her.

"Well, how did you find out?"

"The FBI has been keeping tabs on Larsen's phone. When they overhead his call to this lowlife, they informed us right away.

"I'm going to have one of the Regina police officers escort you home. Peggy, please see that Judy gets home safely."

Freda was still in a celebratory mood. She was not ready for bed. Where was her tablet? She went into the bedroom, where Jose was already sleeping. He had sipped on a few too many beers. She smiled. He was such a good man. She was so happy that he had a chance to relax and meet new friends. She saw her tablet on her night stand. Grabbing it, Freda went to the living room where she sat down to read the news. The headlines were:

RCMP Running Short of Officers for Protection Detail as Threats to Politicians Increases

Storm Brings Rain to British Columbia's Sunshine Coast for First Time in Months

Bill Larsen, PAP Political Organizer Arraigned for Conspiracy to Commit Murder

Canada is Weaving Indigenous Science into Environmental Policy Making

Prime Minister Gervais Announces $500 Million for First Nations and Métis Climate Change Initiatives

Six Million Have Been Displaced by Flooding in Central and West Africa

PART IV

WINTER 2033

27
ALBERTA CLIPPER
REGINA SASKATCHEWAN

Freda had just finished face-timing with family in La Cruces. Everyone here was in their rooms getting ready for bed. It was time to catch up on the news.

She grabbed her tablet. The headlines tonight were:

Mujahideen Forces outside Kabul, Afghanistan, are Threatening the Taliban Government. Attackers feel the Taliban is Becoming too Liberal

War in Eastern Europe is Still at a Stalemate

President Harrison Petry's Private Holdings are Investigated for Tax Fraud

The Patriots of America Party (PAP) is Way Ahead in most Red States, even with the Justice Department's Ongoing Investigation of the President

President Petry's Failed Policies on the Economy and Global Warming Contribute to India Becoming the World's Largest Economy

China Cannot Recover from the Previous Summer of Extreme Heat and Record Rainfalls. Storm Damage to Rural Towns and Villages and Destruction of Crops have Caused Nearly One Million Deaths

Virginia Receives One Billion Dollars in National Rebuilding Funds Passed by Congress and Signed off by the President to Offset the Losses Caused by Flooding Last Summer

New Mexico, with a Democratic State Governor, has been Asking for Similar Funding for its State for the Damage Caused by Forest Fires over the Spring, Summer, and Fall. So far, the PAP-Controlled House and Senate have not Responded

Over night, Saskatchewan can Expect an Alberta Clipper

Freda typed in Alberta Clipper to find out what it is. Wikipedia came on her screen with:

An Alberta Clipper is a major winter-season storm. It strikes in parts of the prairies and central Canadian provinces and the upper midwest United States, Great Lakes, and northeastern portions of the U.S. These storms are associated with cold, dry continental air masses and generate small-scale, short-lived weather events, typically producing 8 to 15 cm of snow in a 3- to 6-hour period.

Hmm, she thought, *what will that mean for us tomorrow?* Never did she think the one on its way would last a whole week.

Overnight, a powerful wind blew in. It howled. Charlie hid in the cellar in a corner. Victoria and Manuel crawled into bed with her and Jose. It had been years since they did that. Camilla climbed in with Mandy.

In the morning, their electric, self-driving car was buried under the snow. Temperatures had plunged. Radio bulletins advised people to stay inside. With the wind chill, it was minus 45 Celsius outdoors. Winds were reported at 100 KM. Frostbite on exposed skin would occur within minutes.

The radio became vital to them. Reports say all Regina schools are closed until further notice, that students can do the assignments posted online. Jose was told not to come into work.

The storm continued to rage all week. It plugged roads and rail lines.

News reports documented the unimaginable hardships to farmers and cattle ranchers. Whiteouts make it difficult for dairy farmers to reach their barns to milk their cows. One farmer called the radio station to inform listeners he had to cut a hole in his barn roof in order to get in and milk his cows. Cattle ranchers reported hundreds of cattle had died from exposure.

Dozens of people died during the week, many of whom were caught in their vehicles when the storm struck. They had left the relative safety of their vehicles to walk for help. Out in the open, they became disoriented due to the reduced visibility. Their frozen bodies were sometimes found within feet of their vehicles.

Freda insisted that everyone stay inside except for letting Charlie step outside the door to do his business. One whole week inside resulted in cabin fever. People were getting on each other's nerves, and sleeping patterns were out of whack. Freda decided to act like a camp counsellor. She had everyone play board games instead of being on their electronic devices all the time. She assigned chores to everyone, like taking turns with Charlie and helping around the house. Jose thought Freda was more like a drill sergeant.

The storm subsided, but the freezing cold temperatures stayed. Jose and Manuel spent hours shovelling the snow away from the house and off the driveway. Just as they finished, a city plough roared past, leaving a hard-packed ridge at the bottom of the driveway. They had to go out again and clear that away. Jose needed to be able to get his car out so that he could go back to work.

The radio reported it was the worst Alberta Clipper ever, leaving four feet of snow in a week with some places having drifts 12 feet high.

And, for the Kirks, it became a weather story to share with their families in New Mexico.

∼

JUDY CALLED Freda from Regina Welcome You. March was approaching.

"How are you, Freda?"

"I never imagined cold like we just had and, for so long," said Freda.

"Our winters are cold, but Freda, the winter is getting shorter every year. Storms like we just had are caused by changing weather patterns.

"Freda, how are your two new girls?"

"Camilla is in grade 5. She's a bright girl. She's speaking English well. Mandy continues to be her big sister and helps her with the language and her school work. There is no information on where she's from, except it's most likely Central America. Canadian authorities tell us it's so difficult since no one has inquired about the murdered family."

"How about Mandy?" asked Judy.

"She's doing well. Her relatives from the south are in contact with her. But she's content here, and she's an adult. She wants to stay here. We've told her she can stay with us as long as she wishes. Her permanent resident card came in. Tim Hortons nominated her under the Provincial Nominee Program. She is now an assistant manager there. Her job pays for her classes at the university. She is taking two courses a semester.

"Our driveway now has two cars in it. Mandy bought a compact car for herself. She also pays room and board. We didn't ask her for it, but she insists."

"Freda, I'm hoping you will do something for me."

"If I'm able, for sure," answered Freda.

Judy explained that Allan would like to interview her about her immigration experience in Canada. He will Zoom with her from an unknown location.

Freda didn't need Jose's permission or the time to decide. She wanted to tell her story. "Yes," she said enthusiastically.

∼

Peter Hamilton approached Sergeant Dagenais and Corporal Jennings outside the courtroom. News cameras were filming his every step.

"Are you happy? Two young Saskatchewan boys are going to spend the best part of their lives behind bars. For what? An incident that got out of hand and resulted in the deaths of some fucking wetbacks. They snuck in. Soon there won't be any real Saskatchewan people living here," shouted Hamilton.

Dagenais' eyes narrowed and he scowled at Hamilton. He nudged Jennings towards the vehicle waiting for them. They got in and drove away.

Reporters tried to get Hamilton to speak with them, but Hamilton just told them to fuck off.

Peter Hamilton was driving back to Willow Bunch. The jury in the first-degree murder trial against his oldest son came back with a guilty plea. His youngest son had been the principal Crown witness. Robert had also been the key witness against Peter's second son, who was also convicted of first-degree murder. Robert had pled guilty on the charge of manslaughter and had received a five-year sentence. He will be eligible for parole in one year's time. The others received life sentences with no chance for parole until they had served a mandatory 25 years.

Peter Hamilton had declared bankruptcy in December of last year. He only had his Willow Bunch home and some cash in the bank.

He was drinking and driving. The roads were slippery, and he was driving fast. It was dark out. The mule deer in the middle of the road froze when the headlights of the Cadillac beamed into its eyes. The car hit the deer, sending it high into the air and through the windshield. The deer landed in Hamilton's lap. The buck's horns sliced into Hamilton's chest and midsection. The vehicle skidded off the road, plowed into the ditch, and settled in a slough. The car floated initially and then slowly sank to the bottom.

It was days before Hamilton's body was found and retrieved from the slough.

The vehicle accident report found its way to the in basket of the RCMP corporal in Coronach. He phoned Corporal Lyle Jennings to tell him about it.

Jennings was numb to the news. Hamilton's death provided him no satisfaction.

28

FREDA'S INTERVIEW
FREDA IN REGINA. WALKER IN VAIL COLORADO

To his listeners, he's still Allan Walker. It's still the most popular podcast in North America.

The FBI had placed him in a French Chateau-styled home near Vale, Colorado. It belongs to a wealthy south Florida couple who use it for ski vacations. The couple had leased it out for a year while they holidayed at another one of their properties at Cap D'Antibes. The FBI rented it under a pseudonym.

The place is enormous. There are six bedrooms, each with its own ensuite. The house is nestled in a valley with hills surrounding it. In the distance, there are snow-capped mountains.

Walker has two FBI agents protecting him at all times, but they provide him with little companionship. As an example,

Colorado legalized marijuana years ago, but neither would join him in sharing a joint.

When he walked outdoors, they came with him. When he shopped in Vale, they drove him. He tried a little fly-fishing. They accompanied him.

They left him alone when he worked on his podcasts. The FBI had permitted Weber to communicate virtually with Judy. That's how arrangements were made to interview Freda Kirk.

"Mom, he's not videoing you; he's recording you. You didn't need to get your hair done and buy a new dress," grumbled Victoria.

Everyone was in the front room where Freda was preparing for her interview with Allan Walker.

"Listen here. I cook, clean, and care for you guys all the time. This is my time, and I'll appear as I wish," Freda defended herself.

"You look beautiful, Freda," piped in Jose. The others all agreed.

"Okay, okay, everyone out except Mandy. She'll help me with the App we'll be using."

They all gave Freda a hug, told her to break a leg, and left her with Mandy.

Mandy touched the icon to connect Freda to Walker. Mandy smiled at Freda and flashed a V sign with her fingers.

"Hello Mrs. Kirk, I'm Allan Walker."

"Very nice to meet you," Freda replied. "Please call me Freda. It makes me nervous to be so formal."

"Fair enough, Freda, and you call me Allan. Please do not feel pressured. No reply is a wrong reply. No answer to my question is a wrong answer. When I have it ready to put on the internet, I will email you your own copy. Now, I'm going to begin with an open question asking how you are in Regina, Saskatchewan, Canada."

"I thank God for his blessing. Regina is a nice place to live except it's freezing in the winter. (Mandy smiled at her answer). But in all honesty, I miss our life in La Cruces. There is no large Mexican-American community here. I miss our family. I miss my friends. Moving, especially to a new country, is hard, very hard."

Walker asked, "Freda, tell my audience why you had to move from the southwestern United States to Canada."

"I'm going to tell you why my husband Jose wanted to come here.

"At La Cruces, New Mexico, the water supply was drying up. He could no longer operate a landscaping business because of mandatory cuts in water. He found an opportunity in Saskatchewan, applied for a job here, and got it. He'd didn't feel we could afford to live in the northern States because the rich were buying up properties there and making it hard for the little guy to move to those places. So he found a job in a place we never knew existed. My Jose is a provider for his family. That's what drives him.

"Now, I'm going to tell you why I wanted to come. It was my idea to move here. I read about why La Cruces was having droughts year after year. I read about why New Mexico was in flames in every season except winter. And, I saw the type of politicians being elected. Ones who cared only about their own interests, who were motivated by payoffs from the fossil industry, and who were indifferent to the people's suffering. These people were not going to be the ones to put an end to the drought and fires.

"And, I decided that, as an undocumented alien, I would be one of the least cared about when people were faced with scarcities because of drought, fires, heat waves, and job losses. Like those politicians, I decided my interests came first. And my primary interest was for me and my family to feel safe somewhere, not having to worry about powerful people taking our security away.

"In my view, America has too much noise and drama. It has more noise now from monster storms, people coughing from polluted air, sirens from police and emergency vehicles, and gunfire. And PAP has normalized the sounds of violence with rhetoric that is so divisive.

"The drama is from the powerful who masquerade as people trying to solve problems but are just perpetuators who benefit from the continuing problems. Fake news, fake overtures, and phony conflict spiels from social media and TV. You know, Allan, I don't have much of an education so I may be wrong in saying this, but I think this is referred to as MEGA politics.

"It's little people like me and my family who die in the crossfire.

"There are lots of problems to solve in the United States. But the country has all these people making up lies and wanting to go back to the 1950s. Well, I was an illegal Mexican in the United States. Those people wanted me deported even though my husband and my children are American citizens and even though I've lived in the United States since I was a child without ever doing a bad thing. I've been afraid over the last number of years since the PAP took control of our government, that officers from the Immigration and Customs Enforcement (ICE) would apprehend me and send me back to Mexico, that one day ICE would stand at my doorstep and remove me from the only place I've ever known.

"Here, I can apply for Canadian citizenship in three years. Since moving to Regina, I am no longer living in fear of being forcibly separated from my family."

Walker responded, "Freda, you are so right. There are so many people in the United States living in that nightmare you describe. Thank you for sharing that with us. Does Canada have that type of noise?"

Freda replied, "No, no, not even close to that. I listen to Saskatchewan News Talk Radio and people complain about the worst roads in Saskatchewan, hospitals needing more capacities because of the increases in population, and other local concerns. But there aren't national media outlets constantly promoting lies, divisions, and revolutions. Where I am—in Regina, folks complain about the federal government and a province called Quebec where everyone needs to speak French, but it never becomes divisive noise.

"I've only been here a short while. But one thing I know, there's hate everywhere. There are people with a sense of entitlement, who think that way because of the colour of their skin. They recently convicted three brothers of murdering a Central American family that had entered Saskatchewan illegally. It was a hate crime."

Walker asked, "Freda, what are things you like about your new city other than that feeling of not being afraid?"

Freda replied, "I mentioned how I really don't like the cold. Remember, it's our first year here, and people tell us it was an easy winter except for one terrible storm. But the cold is not something I like, sorry.

"We haven't experienced the spring yet. But last summer and fall were wonderful, unless the wind is strong. Regina is one of the windiest places in Canada.

"At the beginning of August, the farm fields near Regina are mixtures of gold, blue, and yellow. We didn't go far from the city, but we drove a city road around the outer edges called the Ring Road. That's where we saw this beautiful landscape. And when it's windy, and because it's so flat here, it looks like the waves of an ocean. I love that.

"The sky is always alive here. Some mornings, the sunrise is pinkish-purple. Some evenings there are red streaks across the sky. Some days, white fluffy clouds race across the sky forming pictures as they fly by. The storm-forming thunderhead clouds are dark grey with black patches and are accompanied by thunder, lightning, wind, and pelting rain. Though scary, it is amazing to see. And then there are the northern lights in the winter. The skies glow with green, yellow, blue and red waves of colour.

"We have everything we need. The stores are mostly the same as the ones in La Cruce. The same with chain restaurants. We have them here. And many of our TV channels are broadcast from the U.S. Often, we forget we're in a different country.

"So far, these are my favourite parts of my new home."

Walker asked, "Freda, you haven't mentioned the people. What are Regina people like?"

"We haven't met that many. I guess that's because we spend so much time inside during the winter months. However, we were here last summer and attended events put on by

Regina Welcomes You, but we met other new Canadians there.

"There are so many immigrants. Regina has many visible minorities from around the world. One thing other immigrants tell me is that Canadians want us to be more like them, I guess to assimilate more easily. It's hard for them to understand how much we miss where we came from and that we want to hold onto our past. But we want to learn to be Canadian too.

"Language is a barrier for many immigrants, but not when you come from the States.

"Canadians are tolerant. At least that's what we've been told. That's why I think there's a quieter tone up here. There is not all that background noise caused by strife."

Walker asked, "What are your family challenges in the near future?"

"Buying our own house. We are happy in our rental, but I want a bigger home. Our family has grown from four to six members, and I'd like more space. In New Mexico, we had just built a sprawling home before we had to leave.

"But it's hard to find a home and buy it. The rapid growth in population is pushing prices up. People moving from places like Toronto and Vancouver are loaded with cash from the sale of their million-dollar homes there. Many of the immigrants bring some cash with them, especially the Americans.

We have money, but a new home with four bedrooms in the new neighbourhoods costs nearly $800,000 in Canadian dollars. We would need to get a mortgage. Jose's job does not pay all that much. Interest rates are nearly 6 percent for a mortgage.

"Jose has been thinking about opening his own cleaning business. I could help him with that. Maybe he could keep his job and I could clean homes and hire some other immigrants to help me. Jose knows how to run a business."

The interview touched on Medicare, finding a doctor, and about hospital capacity. When the time allotted for the interview was up, Walker thanked Freda for sharing her time and observations with him and his listeners.

~

PRESIDENT HARRISON PETRY spent his days in the White House consolidating his control of PAP and the majorities it held in Congress. The Democrats introduced Articles of Impeachment in the House of Representatives. The PAP-controlled House stopped the action at once.

Petry stepped up his fight against the Democrats.

"Fake," he yelled into the mike during a meeting with reporters in the Rose Garden. "I've enemies who want to stop me from *Making America Great Again* so they can benefit from the Swamp they call Washington. That recording of a conversation between me and that corrupt man, Bill Larsen, is a fake. And I'm going to find out who leaked it to the media and have that person tried for treason."

Petry continued as President unfettered by truth or convention.

~

Premier Mahon stared fiercely at her partner Sammy Nelson. Photographs were spread across the living room table in front of them. The pictures showed Sammy in a compromised position with another woman.

"What the fuck, Rebecca?" Sammy's eyes flashed. "Where the fuck did you get these?"

Rebecca's mouth twisted. "Is that all you care about? How I got these? Sammy, for someone who's so smart, you're acting pretty stupid right now. I do have a security detail that pokes into my affairs to catch things before they become a problem for me."

Angrily, Sammy lashed out, "You bitch, you dependent bitch! You've been tracking me."

Rebecca gave Sammy a dirty look. "You just think I depend on you. See, you confuse devotion to being clingy. I loved you, love you still, but I hate you right now. I hate you for cheating, but I hate you more because you actually believe I'm no one without you beside me."

"And you're not. You'd still be an NDP member. You have no vision. You've been riding on my coat tails."

"Fine, fine, get out now. You're fired. Fortunately, the Prime Minister has a position in Ottawa for you."

Suddenly contrite, Sammy replied, "Rebecca, I love only you. These affairs are only that. Brief interludes when I needed them to break from our reality."

"And what reality is that? And how can you justify your betrayal to satisfy your lust? That hurts, but your superiority hurts more," said Rebecca.

"The reality is that I need these interludes to function in the crazy world we're living. The reality is that you are always in the spotlight and I'm in the shade. The reality is that, yes, I do lust. When I see someone I'm attracted to, I try to get to know them better."

"Just get out. I've an appointment," stated Rebecca.

29

PRESENT THREATS
OTTAWA ONTARIO

Sammy has moved to Ottawa. She arranged for her mother to live with her there. Provisions are in place for a caregiver to be with her mother when Sammy is not around. And Sammy is not around all that regularly.

After she was fired, Prime Minister Gervais hired Sammy to lead Canada's team in discussions with an American team appointed by the President of the United States to come up with plans to address the growing migration from south to north. Petry had been against the idea one day and then shortly after, proposed it to Gervais so he could tell Americans it was his initiative.

Sammy poured herself into her new job. She picked the Canadian team members and submitted their names to Gervais for cabinet approval.

Her role is a high profile one. They broadcast her name in Canada and the United States. The RCMP security service recommended she have a detail assigned to her. Immigration and climate change are hot topics for the far right. Sammy becomes a target of threats and attacks on far right social media. The fact that she's a lesbian enrages them even more.

Sammy, independent as ever, told the RCMP, "Thank you but no thank you." She has been walking about freely since she was a child. In those days, it was her parents who received the implied threats, "Child Protection will take your child away." Those people in Outlook did not differ much from the crazies who threatened her today.

After Corporal Jennings' work in the Regina Major Crimes Unit, he was promoted to Sergeant and posted to Ottawa. Sergeant Jennings is a team leader on one of the Prime Ministers security details. He was updating her on protection plans and the most urgent threats.

"Our highest alert threat is against Sammy Nelson. I would ask that you order her to comply with our request for her to accept security," said Jennings.

"Sergeant, I will do that."

"Madame Prime Minister, CSIS has intercepted messages on the internet that informs us President Petry has a team of dark web operatives drafting lies about you and your earlier years at McGill. They reflect badly on you if allowed to be released."

"Sergeant, please back channel this information to Director Cousins at the FBI. CSIS can work at preventing what they can. I'm a fighter, and I'll challenge anything untrue that is released."

Gervais's eyes twinkled, "You know, I wasn't a good Catholic girl all the time."

∽

THAT SAME EVENING, Sammy said to her mom, "I'm going out to the pharmacy to pick up some of your prescriptions, Mom. You have your alert system if you need me to come back at once."

Sammy's mother grinned, "My baby girl, have I told you how happy I am to be with you?"

Sammy smiled back, "Mom, you tell me ten times a day. I should tell you the same more often. I'm so happy you are here. Now, show me your alert button so I know you have it handy."

Her mother flipped it up from the side of her chair.

"Sammy, you're still walking everywhere. You're so dear. Be careful. This is a big city. It's not Outlook."

"I will, Mom." Sammy put on her coat and left her high-rise apartment. She took the elevator down to the main floor. The high rise is located on Somerset Street.

She left the building and headed west. It was dark out; there was no one else about. She walked along undisturbed. Suddenly, from an alley along Somerset, a man appeared out of the darkness. Sammy has seen him before but cannot remember where.

The man spoke in a menacing tone, "Hey, dike, you don't have a chair this time. Remember me from the Hotel Saskatchewan? You sure stunk the joint out with all your green this, green that. You cost me a well-paying job on the oil rigs with all that bullshit."

Sammy pressed her lips together then replied, "Look, asshole, get out of here before I kick your ass." They were the last words she ever uttered. Another man had quietly moved behind her and swung a hammer at her temple. She fell to the ground.

The two men dragged her into the alley. Her body was found a couple of hours later by a man walking his dog. He heard the emergency alarm signal and walked towards the sound. Sammy's mother had been pushing the button when her daughter had not returned right away.

EPILOGUE
THE YEAR 2037

Freda is on her tablet reading the news. It's quieter in the home they had purchased in Harbour Landing two years earlier. The University had promoted Jose to a managerial job, and he makes decent money. Freda did not find work. She has been too busy with her children.

Mandy is a high school teacher. She paid her own way through school by working for years at Tim Hortons. Victoria and Camilla will graduate from high school soon. Manuel is interested in the trades. He takes a lot of shop classes.

On her tablet, she read the following headlines:

Former Political Operative Bill Larsen Found Dead in Prison Cell from Apparent Heart Attack

Majority Democrats in House and Senate Move Forward with Articles of Impeachment Against President Petry, the Longest Serving American President

Russia Sues for Peace with Eastern European Neighbours. Nearly Five Million Died in 16-year Conflict

China's Ambitions in Southeast Asia Are Being Curtailed by Most Unlikely Countries, Pakistan and India

It's the final headline that she drills down to read the entire story.

California's Vast Central Valley is Under Water. Millions Flee Flooding

"In California's Central Valley, the heavy rain started coming down and has continued now for three days

A rancher in the valley just below the Sierra Nevada reports that rain poured on the mountains and drained into rivers, streams and creeks coming down from higher elevations. On the lower ground, where the water flows into the river, the river banks overflowed and spread out. The water rose and started forming vast lakes that covered large parts of the Central Valley.

The same draining and flooding started on the west side of Central Valley, where the Coastal mountains rise above the valley.

Flash flooding took a lot of life. People awoke to the danger but could not escape. Others, who had an earlier warning, fled to higher land.

The Valley is home to nine million people. The Valley produces 25% of America's food supply.

California has enacted a state of emergency. But this weather disaster is near impossible to curb. The rain just keeps falling. There are more human deaths, dead livestock floating on these large bodies of water, and crops are destroyed everywhere.

California's capital Sacramento is under water. They evacuated the city. It's the second time in the last 165 years the city has been flooded. In 1862, northern California, southern Oregon and eastern Nevada were flooded for two months in the winter. Like this current rainfall, the abundant rainfall had been because of higher local temperatures than usual. Unlike 1862, the higher temperatures have been ongoing for years now. The human casualties exceeded 4,000 people.

Dr. Juan Moreno, a renowned climatologist at USC, is warning governments that the rain may fall for weeks. He says this rainfall is resulting from what is called an atmospheric river. An atmospheric river is a narrow, fast-flowing stream of moist air, many thousands of kilometres long, and a few thousand kilometres wide. It travels as fast as 45 KM per hour. A cooling-down period preceded the rainfall.

Dr. Moreno says to officials that this rainfall will cause more damage than the one in 1862. It covers a far greater area and the mountains surrounding the valley are almost bare of trees due to forest fires and insect damage caused by many years of drought.

∼

Prime Minister Gervais was chewing on a cucumber sandwich, her favourite lunch. Her assistant told her who was on the line. She grimaced and then took the receiver.

"Hello Mr. President, congratulations on your re-election. Yes, your comeback is remarkable. What can I do for you?"

Loud noise at the other end. Gervais held the phone away from her ear.

"Yes, sir, our crowded mutual border is a concern."

More loud noise. Blah, Blah, Blah.

Gervais, a corner of her mouth lifted, responds. "There are one million people at the border wanting to come here. We need to process their applications. Waiting time is now about a year. It's the California flooding that has sent many Americans to our border wanting to move here."

More loud noise. The man calls her Pauline, so she becomes informal with him.

"Harrison, it's the United States responsibility to care for its citizens, and no, Canada will not pay for the needs of the people located in your country and living on your soil while awaiting entry to Canada."

Noise, almost screaming at the other end. Gervais banged the receiver in her hand on her desk. She remembered what Sammy had advised her to do. It worked. The man stopped screaming at his end.

"Sorry Harrison, the phone fell out of my hands. The United States isn't the only country with climate change issues. We've had thousands die during the summer from heat waves, tornados, and floods. But I think we are addressing the greenhouse gas, and our population is mostly behind our initiatives and investments."

Blah, blah, blah from the buffoon.

Gervais spoke, tongue in cheek, "Wasn't your re-election motto *Go North*? I know your rich friends are going north in your country, but what did you expect the people who don't have the money to go north once your friends bought out everything? They are coming north to Canada."

Shouting, anger, swearing. Click. The line went dead.

"Please send Inspector Jennings in," requested the Prime Minister.

Jennings said, "Madame Prime Minister, there's a significant increase in right-wing hate mail for you. This is an example." He handed her the note.

You stupid fucking anti-freedom pro kill shot, ugly fucking wrench. Where the FUCK do you get off spewing the garbage you do? You fucking evil parasite worm. I pray to God that he brings his wrath on you and that Premier cunt running Saskatchewan. After I deal with the Saskatchewan cunt, I will personally come for you. I'll cut you up in pieces and throw your remains to the pigs.

Signed,

A True Canadian - A Free Male in Canada

"Do you think he votes for my party?" laughed Gervais.

"Madame Prime Minister, these threats have to be taken seriously. Right-wing extremism is growing. You're one of their favourite targets. You will have to comply with our more rigorous security."

"I will."

The End

ACKNOWLEDGMENTS

All my books have resulted from a considerable contribution from friends and family. My wife, Vivian, has dedicated her skills and time to all of my books since I started writing. I can say the same about James Pridham, who has been the creative designer of most of my book covers and ad designs. Thank you!

Murray Letts, Stephen Duggan and Allan Walker read my drafts and provided their insights on how to make the story better for readers. I thank them for this.

And of course, I thank Gina Jestadt, owner of Joose Publishing, for her continuing support and skills in publishing my books. If there are writers out there who do not know about self-publishing, I encourage them to reach out to Gina. You will not be sorry.

ABOUT THE AUTHOR

Keith Landry is the author of 14 very popular Canadian stories that tell history in a storytelling way. He only started writing three (3) years ago, at age 69. Keith hopes his stories informs his readers of past events that shaped our country and still influence us today.

Keith has a unique writing style. He picks interesting news articles from our past and uses them as the underlying basis for his stories. These news articles are skillfully woven into a narrative brought about by the human interest of the characters.

Keith lives with his wife, Vivian, in Regina, Saskatchewan.

Here is some praise for Keith Landry's books

"Keith Landry takes us back in time by skillfully using newspaper reports of the day. Landry showcases the brilliant writing of Canadian newspaper men (I believe all the reporters were men, as were all the police, lawyers, jurists and other authority figures).

Building on the bare bones reporting that might please even Ernest Hemmingway, Landry brings us to a world where men totally dominated every aspect of Canadian life. The first story takes us back to the turn of the last century, long before women could even vote."

"A trip down a chilling memory lane with original accounts by Ottawa Valley reporters writing about heinous murders many decades ago."

"I love all his books, so well researched and spell binding. I like how he intertwined a love story into the script. How about making this into a movie or theatre production?"

"Living in Saskatchewan, I have heard about "Black Tuesday" off and on for years, but never actually had a vivid "picture" of what took place. This book is definitely a vivid portrait of dismal treatment of the miners, their insurrection and the horrific events of September 29, 1931. I now have mental images of that sad and horrific day."

"I loved this book . It gives the reader an uncomfortable look at the Prairies in the 1930's. Uncomfortable because we learn how poorly Canadians were treated by companies....not something that we want to be reminded of or made aware of for the first time. The mistreatment that the miners experienced at the hands of the mine owners and operators was soften by the narrative of the love story.

The author has well researched the events of the time. The history of rural Saskatchewan and the developing relationship between a local women and wealthy oil man from Calgary keeps us turning the pages."

"Master storyteller Keith Landry has done it again. His innate ability to lay words down on paper as if his pen and paper are brush and canvas, shines through in this compilation of Canadian Catastrophes.

Mr. Landry's amicable modus operandi offers the reader an opportunity to travel back in time while enjoying, an adventurous excursion, criss-crossing Canada.

Easy reading at its best."

"This is a story I read about in a local paper and could not wait to read. I had always heard a story that there was a man hanged in the jail in my home town. This was the story. Growing up in this area nobody ever talked to me about the details. Landry's writing style brings the reader into the small towns in an historical journey. He brings life to the central characters - the accused, the investigators and their families. A must read for anybody interested in true historical crimes, especially if you're from the Ottawa Valley."

"Landry books are books you can't put down."

ALSO BY KEITH LANDRY

Allumette Island Massacre

Dalpe's Crime Chronicles

Dalpe and the Nazi

Dalpe and the Communist Spies

Dalpe and the Missing Men

Dalpe and the Roots of Evil

The Boarding School at the end of the Dirt Road

Murder Tales from the Archives

Murder Tales in the Ottawa Valley

All Roads Lead to Campbell's Bay

Motley Crooks

Black Tuesday A Canadian Love Story

Canadian Catastrophes

Broken Bottle

www.amazon.com/author/keithlandry

Manufactured by Amazon.ca
Acheson, AB